I0746080

MARY CRAWFORD

Love is More than Skin Deep

HIDDEN HEARTS BOOK 4

COPYRIGHT

© 2016 Mary Crawford. All rights reserved. No portion of this book may be reproduced in any form or by any electronic or mechanical means including information storage and retrieval systems – except in the case of brief quotations in articles or reviews – without permission in writing from its publisher, Mary Crawford and Diversity Ink Press.

This novel is a work of fiction. Names, characters, businesses, places, events and incidents are either the products of the author's imagination or used in a fictitious manner. Any resemblance to actual persons, living or dead, or actual events is purely coincidental.

All brand names and product names used in this book are trademarks, registered trademarks, or trade names of their respective holders. I'm not associated with any product or vendor in this book.

Published on August 27, 2016, by Diversity Ink Press and Mary Crawford. Publisher may be reached at MaryCrawfordAuthor.com.

ISBN: 978-1-945637-31-5

Covers by Covers Unbound.

HIDDEN BEAUTY SERIES

Until the Stars Fall from the Sky
So the Heart Can Dance
Joy and Tiers
Love Naturally
Love Seasoned
Love Claimed
If You Knew Me (and other silent musings) (novella)
Jude's Song
The Price of Freedom (novella)
Paths Not Taken
Dreams Change (novella)
Heart Wish (100% charity release)
Tempting Fate
The Letter
The Power of Will

HIDDEN HEARTS SERIES

Identity of the Heart
Sheltered Hearts
Hearts of Jade
Port in the Storm (novella)
Love is More Than Skin Deep
Tough
Rectify
Pieces (a crossover novel)
Hearts Set Free
Freedom (a crossover novel)
The Long Road to Love (novella)
Love and Injustice (Protection Unit)
Out of Thin Air (Protection Unit)
Soul Scars (Protection Unit)

OTHER WORKS:
The Power of Dictation
Vision of the Heart
#AmWriting: A Collection of Letters to Benefit The
Wayne Foundation

DEDICATION

This book is dedicated to Judy Noble Cloud.

May those nineteen pictures you chose to share

while you were baring your soul to the world

start an awareness campaign bigger than your dreams

and save more lives than anyone can count.

Thank you for allowing me to use your

story as the vehicle to write mine.

FOREWORD

My journey with skin cancer began over twenty years ago, in 1995. It was mainly a private journey, until the Fall of 2015. In September 2015, I had cancerous areas removed in what was my most invasive surgery to date. During the three-hour surgery, I had 23 places removed, ten by excision (meaning I had ten places on me that had stitches) and thirteen by laser. I was immobile for two weeks following the surgery, and I continue to have lasting effects from the skin cancer and surgery.

A month after that surgery, I made a private post on my Facebook page with a narrative of what I had been through with the surgery and recovery process and included pictures of me during various stages of recovery. A friend urged me to make the post public so he could share it, and after initially resisting, I agreed. What subsequently transpired was incredible – people shared the post, their friends shared the post, and businesses shared the post. Eventually, media outlets around the world picked up the post, and a local news station aired my story. People were talking about and becoming more informed about skin cancer – a cancer that although is the most common cancer in the United States, tends to remain relatively low on people's radar.

It was through the sharing of the Facebook post that Mary Crawford saw it. Mary contacted me in February 2016 and asked if she could use my story as a storyline for one of her characters in an upcoming book. Mary explained that she donates 15% of her profits from each book to charity and that I would be allowed to choose the charity for this novel. I was thrilled that Mary wanted to help further awareness regarding skin cancer, and I am honored to choose The Skin Cancer Foundation (www.skincancer.org) as the charity for this book.

My hope is that you take good care of your skin – your future self will thank you. And I hope you enjoy *Love is More Than Skin Deep*!

Judy Noble Cloud

Chapter One

Shelby

Gripping my idea folder in my hand, I pause at the front door of Ink'd Deep. I can't believe I'm being such a chicken about this. This isn't even my first tattoo. This cool chick, Delaney Jane, gave me my first one a couple months ago when I first found out I would be part of a traveling teacher program this summer. Unfortunately, she told me that the design I want on my back is not the type of work she does, so she passed me off to one of her colleagues. I hope whoever takes me on is as chill as she is. Delaney Jane and I clicked and I'm afraid to trust someone new. I've heard that a piece as large as the one I want to get hurts a lot more than the tiny compass on my ankle bone. I take a deep breath and try to center myself. You know what they say — nothing ventured nothing gained. If it hurts a bit, it will be a reminder of all the things I have gone through to get the piece of paper which was the impetus for this tattoo.

I smile to myself. *That's right. I earned a Masters Degree all by myself with nobody's help.* I did it when no one thought I'd be able to accomplish anything remotely close. So, what's a little needle and ink on my skin? I can accomplish anything.

As I step into the shop, I'm struck by the vibe here. It's distinctly masculine, but as always, there is a clear feminine heartbeat running through the whole business. A statuesque young woman walks toward me, her hair is ink black and down to her waist. I feel a tinge of envy. My hair is more like Ramen noodles. I've tried hair straighteners and flat irons to no avail. I went through a stage in high school where I tried to look like everyone else and all I ended up doing was frying my hair. If one more person calls me pocket-sized, I think I'll go insane. Although being small was handy when I was younger, it doesn't do me any favors now. It's mortifying to have two college degrees and still be offered the children's menu at a restaurant.

The woman extends her hand to me and greets, "Hello, welcome to Ink'd Deep, I'm Rogue Macklin. How can I help you?"

"Umm… Hi, I'm Shelby Lyons… Um… I think I'd like to get a tattoo of a dream catcher on my back," I blurt as I let go of the death grip I've got on my idea folder and place it in front of her.

"You must be DJ's client. She said you were all sorts of fun to work with. It's nice to meet you. I can't wait to see your ideas. I love drawing dream catchers."

"Really? Delaney seemed a tad freaked out by my design," I reveal.

"I think it's a matter of perspective, I love detail work and color. DJ hasn't had quite as much time in the chair as I have. She'll get more confident with stuff outside her wheelhouse after a while. She prefers to focus on old-school black and white art. The piece she did on your ankle is top-notch work, though."

I grin at her as I respond, "It is, isn't it? The 3-D effect is spot on. Some people actually reach out to touch it like it's real."

Rogue pulls out a couple of my drawings and compares them. "What do you have going on here?"

"See the watercolor effect in the drawing with the orange? I want this style, but I'd it to be more blue, teal and purple. Is it possible? Can I combine two designs like that?" I ask, hopefully.

Rogue shrugs as she pulls out a fresh sheet of paper and some colored pencils and takes some notes. "Shelby, it's your tattoo, you tell me what *you* want. Close your eyes for a moment and tell me about the things which make you happy."

I start to let my eyes drift shut, but the analytical part of me rears its ugly head and I pop my eyes open and ask for clarification, "Any ol' random thing or just stuff I like that's related to the tattoo?"

Rogue chuckles. "I'll get more specific later, but right now I simply need to know what gives you the warm-fuzzies."

I draw a deep breath and let it out as I do when I'm meditating. I choose a dragonfly wind chime which is hanging from the ceiling as my focal point and try to clear my mind from everything negative. When I first started this stuff, it sounded hokey to me, but it kind of works. I take a deep breath and try to flood my brain with all the things I like. "My favorite thing in the whole wide world is old worn Levi jeans, warm from the dryer. I love lilac trees and kids finger-painting during summer vacation. I like tie-dyed shirts, Skittles and blowing big bubbles with bubblegum. I like walking through fields and blowing on dandelions."

The bell over the door rings and jolts me out of my happy bubble. An arresting man with short-cropped black hair and an angular face acknowledges me with a nod and a brief smile. For a moment, I actually forget how to breathe. Apparently, it's not just me. Rogue notices my reaction and grins. "I don't know about you, but if it were me, I would put that man on my 'happy list.'"

"It would be nice if we could go shopping for them that way, wouldn't it?" I smirk. "Unfortunately, love has to be a two-way street and guys like him are rarely, if ever, interested in me. Most of them think I'm the kid babysitter from down the street. I recently graduated from my Masters program — that's why I'm celebrating with a tattoo. Most guys like him are already situated in their careers. They want someone far more successful than me."

Rogue laughs out loud. "I used to think that way too, until I accidentally married a software mogul."

"How did you accidentally marry him?" I puzzle, trying to figure out what she means.

"Wait, I didn't actually mean that the way it sounds. I didn't accidentally marry him — I accidentally fell in love. When we first met, I wasn't even sure he wasn't scamming me because he was trying to tell me I was somebody I wasn't — or at least I thought I wasn't. Then, he was trying to give me money and expensive gifts all the time," she explains. "Who does that? It took me a while to figure it all out but by the time I did, it was too late, I was already head over heels in love with him. So, that's how I fell in love with a software developer who has more money than anyone I've ever met."

"Were you rich too?" I ask, my curiosity getting the better of me.

"Oh, Geez, no! I grew up on food stamps and visiting the food bank. My mom tried incredibly hard, but she was a single mom and sometimes the ends just didn't meet."

"Was it hard to get used to your new lifestyle?" I'm fascinated by her rags-to-riches story. I've read books with this storyline and seen it in movies, but I've never actually met someone who experienced it.

Rogue gives me a small smile. "It definitely grows on you."

Rogue tears a piece of paper off the tablet she's been working on and holds it up for me to see. I didn't even realize she's been drawing the whole time we've been talking. It's like she pulled the picture out of my imagination. Her drawing is better than anything I brought in — it's floaty and free with movement. It's simply perfect.

"How do we get your drawing from there to here?" I point to my back.

"I'll make a stencil for the rings, and freehand the rest. How ticklish are you?"

"I don't know. I haven't had to rate myself against other people. I guess my ribs are tender," I shrug.

"I suppose we'll see. Do you need to go to the changing room?"

"I think I'm good," I reply as I shrug off the jean jacket to reveal my leather halter top. It ties at the neck and at my waist leaving my entire back bare. Although it used to belong to my mom in the late 80s, it leaves a great deal to be desired in the modesty department. I cross my arm over my chest as I sit up, mindful of all the alarmingly handsome guys who tend to wander around the tattoo shop. However, a quick look around confirms none of them are paying me any mind. I have a quick mental laugh at my own expense. I should've expected as much.

Rogue returns to the chair with a tray of colors and brightly colored gloves on. She studies me quickly and queries, "Ready?" She gestures for me to lie down on her bench. "Lie face down, please. Your arms can be in any position you'd like until I ask you to move. Any questions?"

Suddenly, an attack of nerves hits and I blurt, "On a scale of one to ten — how bad will this hurt?"

"Pain is an individual thing, I've had young women in here do fine with traditionally tough spots like ribs and the top of the feet and I've had big tough biker dudes practically fainting from pain over run-of-the-mill tattoos. DJ said you were a real trooper with your ankle tattoo, so I don't expect you to have any trouble with this one."

"Okay, I'll try to focus on something other than the pain. I'm just being a wimp, I know."

"Don't beat yourself up too much, back pieces are daunting. Marcus is all kinds of upset with me because I don't have one yet. Everybody here thinks it's funny that I'm a tattoo artist, but I don't have any substantial work yet. Before I was married, it was because I used to do modeling on the side and having no tattoos made it easier for me to book work, but now it's simply because I'm waiting for the perfect inspiration to strike me."

I climb on the table and lie face down before I

mumble into the pillow, "Wow, I thought everybody who worked at a place like this was covered in tattoos — but I understand what you mean about inspiration. My pieces mean something specific to me."

"You mentioned you were celebrating good news?" Rogue probes.

I smile as I brag, "Yeah, I received confirmation today that I've officially earned my Masters Degree in Elementary Education with an emphasis in Mathematics and Special Ed."

A wave of sadness overtakes me as I realize Rogue, a perfect stranger, is the first person I've actually told my good news to. I have no one else left. Wow. I mean, I guess I was aware I'm alone in the world. Still, to put it in such stark terms, that on the happiest day I've had so far in my life, I've got no one to share it with except a random stranger who's going to draw pretty pictures on my skin. That's just sad. *Good way to bum yourself out, Shel.*

I'm confused and a little embarrassed when Rogue hops up on her chair and announces in a loud voice, "I have good news over here at Station Four! What do we do at Ink'd Deep if someone has good news?"

Everyone in the whole tattoo place starts to whistle, applaud and stomp their feet. "We celebrate!"

"What's the good news, Ro?" a guy covered in tattoos asks.

"Marcus, I'm glad you asked. My extremely bright client — who incidentally I share with DJ, is planning to teach math to elementary school kids. She just earned her Master's degree. Let us ring the bell of prosperity and success."

Marcus reaches above his head and rings an old

firehouse bell.

"I'm ringing this three times for good luck," he explains. When he finishes, everyone in the place stands up to give me an ovation. I've never had a standing ovation before. Ever.

During all the chaos, I managed to sit up and wrap a towel around myself. I am looking around the shop in absolute amazement as everyone is still clapping and smiling at me. The guy with the movie-star-good-looks is watching me intently. When I catch him studying me, he smiles at me and gives me a small salute.

Rogue hops down off the chair and grins at me as she declares, "That was fun. I haven't done it in a while. Last time I used the bell, a woman was letting her husband know that they were expecting triplets. He wasn't so sure it was good news."

"It's definitely the first time anything like this has ever happened to me. When I graduated from my undergraduate program, I just got my diploma in the mail. Nobody knew it except me. It was kind of a bummer. I ate a frozen TV dinner by myself in my apartment watching reruns of *Millionaire Matchmaker.*"

"Next time you have good news, you'll have to stop by here. We do good news justice around here —"

"I'm not sure what's next, I'm going to do a traveling teaching program for a while. I'm headed to the Ninth Ward in Louisiana for a couple months this summer. I don't know if it'll turn into a job; I suppose it could. I don't know if they can afford to pay me. I need to eat and pay back student loans."

"Oh, I so understand where you're coming from. Before I met Tristan, I was doing college on the one-course-at-a-time plan. I'm still working on finishing my degree." She pauses for a moment before asking, "Do you mind if I call a colleague over? I'm having a bit of trouble with positioning your stencil."

"No, go right ahead. I'll just grab a little water," I respond. I'm confused because Rogue seemed so sure of herself, she didn't seem at all timid like Delaney Jane. I saw her portfolio on the website. I know she's not a beginner by any stretch of the imagination.

When I see them walking in my direction, I lie back down and stretch out. I'm disconcerted by the grim expression on Rogue's face. The mirth and lightheartedness from a few moments ago has vanished. I wonder if I said something to offend her, I can't imagine what it would have been. She didn't seem upset I'm going to Louisiana.

"Sorry to keep you waiting, I'd like Jade to take a look at your back, if that's all right with you," Rogue explains. "This is Jade, my boss."

"Oh, I wasn't waiting long. I used to spend longer than this in tanning beds. It was nice to have a moment to myself. I've been busy with graduation. I haven't really had a chance to even stop and think about things. I've got so much to do before my trip to Louisiana that my head hurts even thinking about it." I go silent as I realize I'm babbling.

"Shelby, do you mind if I look at your back?" Jade asks.

"I don't have a problem with that. Go ahead and do whatever it is that you need to do."

Rogue uncovers me and begins talking about me, "I noticed the area right above where her bra strap would be. That's the most acute, but she's got a few others with inconsistent texture. They don't appear to be painful because I touched them with my stencil pen and she didn't seem to react," Rogue tells her boss.

Jade changes out her gloves to another set of neoprene gloves. I can feel her running her hands over my back. Eventually, she looks over at Rogue and nods slightly.

"What do you mean?" I ask, my panic level rising. "It's usually not this hard for me to get a tattoo. Is it because I chose a dream catcher? Is there some sort of religious prohibition against it?"

"No, not that I know of," Rogue replies, in the weird tone parents use when they're about ready to give you bad news. "Shelby, based on our experience, we think you should see a doctor about your back. There seems to be something unusual going on."

"What do you mean, 'based on your experience'? What happened? I thought you hadn't even started tattooing yet." I hammer them with a barrage of questions.

Jade shifts, uncomfortably and it seems like she's not wanting to answer my question, but then she says, "We see lots of skin every day and we see a lot of different stuff. We think it might be a good idea to play it safe and have it checked out. Hopefully it's nothing."

"Are you saying you can't tattoo the dream catcher on my back?" I repeat, still bewildered.

"I think perhaps what she's saying is right now the timing isn't right," Tall Cute Guy interjects.

"You don't even know me. What could you possibly know about my life?" I ask, somewhat rhetorically, stunned he has an opinion about my life.

"I know nothing — except you can't change what will be," he pronounces with scary authority.

CHAPTER TWO

MARK

I REALLY WISH I would've stayed in bed this morning. Oh wait, I couldn't because the TV was blaring loud enough to drown out jet engines on a military base. *Darn, why couldn't those wireless headphones work for Ketki?* It's always so hit-and-miss with her. She had one set of headphones which didn't seem to bother her, but after those broke, I've been sorry-outta-luck. I even wrote to the manufacturer of the crazy things to see if they could help me locate more. They wrote me a form letter telling me their stock was limited to what they had on hand and they helpfully included a coupon for newer models. Newer models don't help me. Clearly, they don't understand what it's like to be a single parent of a child with autism.

My day continued to deteriorate rapidly. After I got to work this morning, I found out we lost a case we should've won on summary judgment because the new associate I've been mentoring missed a filing deadline. Garrett Treadwell may think he is God's gift to the legal community, but he might want to nail down the basics first. The person we were representing was in dire need of those years of back pay.

When my buddies and I formed Hunters Crossing,

LLC right out of law school, we had stars in our eyes. We would be the law firm which took cases solely on the merits of the case and not be driven by money. We'd take the cases other firms turned away and just plan to work harder. Well, that part of our plan worked out; we do work ridiculously hard. The frighteningly high burnout rate among our lawyers is simply the cost of having a reputation for taking clients no one else will take.

Of the group of nine of us who started the firm, there are only three left. I have a note on my desk informing me that the Associate Partners would like to meet with the Senior Partners to talk about restructuring the client load. I can read between those lines easily enough. They want us to take on a more profitable caseload and change the focus of our firm. As the longest serving attorney in the firm, I see the financials. From a practical standpoint, I can't say they are wrong — but my heart and mind are telling me two very different things.

At the moment, my stomach is telling me I'm hungry — I have been on the run all day and basically I've forgotten to eat. Unfortunately, I'm busy getting drawn on at the moment and there's nothing I can do about it. Of course, it might be the reason I'm standing around talking like a stupid fortune cookie.

The woman with hair the color of wheat in the fall awkwardly looks up at me with bright blotches of color in her cheeks as she challenges me and my interruption into the conversation. It's then my brain catches up with my feet and my mouth. *Smooth move, Littleson.* Up until this moment, it didn't occur to me I was violating her personal space — I was merely following Jade around the large over-sized studio. Of course she might not have a shirt on — she's getting a back piece done. Great! Now I look like a complete jerk.

On impulse, I kneel down beside her. "You're right. I inserted myself where I didn't belong. I owe you an apology. Good luck with your new degree. If I can be of any assistance, let me know."

Her eyes widen and her mouth forms an O. "How unusual. I don't know if I've ever gotten a straight up apology before. Hello, my name is Shelby."

"Hi, Shelby. I'm Mark."

"Well, Mark, as awkward as this is, I can't say I'm sorry to meet you."

"Wait … how will I find you again?" I ask, against my better judgment.

"I'll be the teacher with the gorgeous dream catcher on my back," she responds with a teasing laugh.

"How did Stage One go for you, Mark?" Jade examines my back.

"On the whole, I would say you radically undersold the itching part."

"Did you use the tattoo care kit we gave you?"

"Yes, I want to thank you. It's the most interactive and engaged I've seen my daughter in a long time. Usually, she has a hard time touching others, but she was so intrigued by the new design on my back that she didn't have any trouble putting on rubber gloves and rubbing on the ointment. She thought it was great fun to trace the new design on my back with her fingers and because of the swelling it had ridges. They made it even more fascinating for her."

"That's interesting. I've heard all kinds of uses for tattoos, but a therapy device is a new one even for me. We'll have to introduce her to Marcus with all of his piercings. He would keep her busy for a while. I've heard Rogue hid a Power Puff Girl somewhere among all of his pieces, as a tribute to an inside joke between them."

"Does she often make tattoos without the client's knowledge?" I ask skeptically.

"Oh, Rogue would never give a tattoo without the express permission of the client, even for Marcus. Marcus actually told her she could do it."

After a few minutes of work, Jade comments, "If your daughter loved your tattoo before, she'll go bananas for it now. This is spectacular if I do say so myself."

"Are you done already?" I ask, surprised at her speed.

"Don't you wish?" Jade replies laughing. "Hold your horses. I only have the first row of feathers done. It will be quite some time before we're finished."

"Can we take a few? I need to check on Ketki. She's with a new sitter." I cringe when I see the time.

Jade shrugs. "Sure not a problem. Just let me know when you want to start back in."

The bell to the shop rings. Rogue and Jade look up. I'm a little surprised they have a customer this late. Jade agreed to work on my back in the evening because I've been in trial this week and things have been crazy at work. I get the impression they weren't expecting anyone either.

Much to my surprise it's Shelby. Well, it's a Shelby-like person. All the light and happiness is gone from her. She's wearing grief as if it's a garment. It's all I can do to stay seated in the tattoo chair. I struggle to remember the lessons I learned the last time I tried to insert myself into a situation where I didn't belong. It's odd. I feel the need to go over and protect her. Protect her from what, I'm not sure — just looking at her brings every male instinct I have to the surface.

Rogue reaches her first. "Shelby, are you okay?"

Shelby drops her purse on the floor and then collapses cross-legged on the floor right beside it. She draws her legs up toward her chest. She looks up at Rogue and answers in a voice choked with tears, "No, I'm not okay. The scary thing is I may never be okay."

Jade leaves her tattooing station and sits down beside Shelby on the floor. "What do you mean?"

Shelby looks at Rogue and Jade. "You guys should really take this show on the road. It turns out you were right to be worried. I have Melanoma — you know, skin cancer. That spot on my back where my bra strap goes, is where my worst lesion is. They are not sure how deep they'll have to cut or how much tissue they will have to cut away. My doctor did warn that it might involve skin grafts and muscle removal."

"I'm so sorry, Shelby. We definitely did not want to be correct," replies Rogue with a profoundly sad expression.

"The doctor said I should be grateful you spotted it because the earlier they find it, the better. I apologize, but I can't find a good side to this. I had to withdraw from my teaching program —" Shelby breaks off with a sob as she gracefully gets up from the floor in one motion. She holds up her hands as if to block any incoming words. "I'm sorry, I just wanted to let you guys know what happened." Shelby spins on the ball of her foot and rushes out the back door.

"Oh my God! I feel awful. Maybe I shouldn't have said anything and waited to tell her until after the summer was over," theorizes Rogue.

Jade touches me on the shoulder. "Mark, do you mind? I need to go talk to her. I think this is the first time Rogue has been involved in one of these and they're always devastating. I want to make sure she doesn't blame herself, whatever the outcome."

"That's understandable. It's all right, I'm free all night."

Jade and Rogue walk out of the room leaving me alone with my thoughts. Normally, this would not be a terribly hazardous thing to do; I generally have them under pretty firm control. However, recently my thoughts seem to stray toward a waif of a woman with a determined spirit and infectious laugh. Shelby looks so crushed today. It would be irresponsible of me not to check on her, right?

Even as I think that thought, my phone buzzes to remind me of the meeting I have at Ketki's school tomorrow. We have to go over her placement for next year; I want to keep Ketki in a mainstream classroom with her peers in a more normal setting, but the school district would like her to be in a more restrictive classroom. Of course they would. It takes a lot of effort to get through to my daughter, but that doesn't mean she's not a brilliant kid behind all of her triggers, meltdowns and hand flaps. If they continue to treat her like she's stupid, she's going to get frustrated and quit trying. I want them to be more creative. Why not put her with older kids who have computer skills? I don't want Ketki to quit the game of life before she's had a chance to play.

This all begs the question as to why I'm even

considering taking on one more problem? The answer is clear. It's who I am — the solver of problems. As much as I hate to admit it, it's pretty much that simple. I can't walk away from a damsel in distress and Shelby looks very distressed. I need to go figure out what's going on.

I expect to find her at the little patio belonging to the bistro next door. It's a favorite hangout for all the Ink'd Deep customers. I'm a little shocked when I don't see her there. There's really no other place she could go from the back door. I am about to turn around and go back inside when I hear the sound of muffled cries from the other side of the dumpster. Alarmed, I cautiously walk around the dumpster as I pick up a two by four in case I have to discourage some lowlifes.

I am completely astounded when I find Shelby sitting on a curb next to the dumpster.

"*Immokalee*, what are you doing out here? Are you okay?"

"*I'mma* what?" she asks. "Did you just cuss me out?"

I throw my head back and laugh. "No, far from it," I explain. "*Immokalee* means tumbling water in Cherokee. Your amazing laugh is the first thing I noticed about you. It reminds me of the sound of rushing water in spring. I started calling you *Immokalee* in my head before I knew what your name was. I guess it just kind of stuck."

"Wow! I should mark this day down in my diary. It's not every day I have an obnoxiously handsome guy whisper sweet nothings to me in a foreign language. It's right out of a Rob Reiner movie." She tries to hide her embarrassment.

It's my turn to be uncomfortable. "I don't know about all of that. I call them as I see them. What are you doing down there on the ground? You can't be comfortable down there. Come join me at a table."

Shelby looks up at me with the bleakest eyes I've seen in a while. "I don't think I should do that. I've waited tables before and trust me: restaurants really prefer paying customers. It will be a while before I can afford to be a paying customer again."

I pull my pants legs up so I can squat down and sit down beside her. She regards me with horror as she insists, "You can't sit down here! You'll ruin your suit."

"Since I really want to talk to you, and I'm thirsty — how about we compromise? You can join me at the table and I'll get you something to drink."

Shelby's brow furrows as she considers my offer. "I almost hate to point this out, but that's not a compromise. You're just being pushy."

"As it so happens, you're right. Then again, so am I — if the ground isn't a good place for me, it's not a good place for you either. Come on, join me for a treat. I would feel guilty if I ate it all by myself. The last time I was in here, Jade was waxing poetically about the strawberry milkshakes over here, but I didn't have time to stop. I was planning to change that today; don't make me feel bad for my indulgence."

Shelby tilts her head as if in deep thought. "Strawberry? As in fresh strawberries?"

I nod. "That's my understanding."

"I guess if my life is going to go to hell in a hand basket, I might as well make the journey with a full stomach."

Shelby's eyes open comically wide when I return to the table. She probably has cause. I may have accidentally ordered burgers and fries with the shakes.

"What is all this?" she asks suspiciously, "You said nothing about buying dinner."

"I decided on the fly. It was actually cheaper to buy the combo meals than to buy the shakes separately. I, for one, am starving and I thought you might be too. This just seemed like the better strategy."

Shelby's eyes gain a faraway glazed over look as she tears up. "Strategy. What a funny word that is. It implies we might be in control of something in our lives. I used to think that was true. I had all these grand plans about how I would live my life and make everyone's lives around me better. Now, I may not live until Christmas. How about them apples? How does a person strategize for cancer?"

"I don't think you strategize for any of it. This isn't like a courtroom, this is just life. Sometimes what we thought was up is down and what we thought was down is up."

Shelby takes a couple bites of her hamburger. "That's all nice and philosophical and all, but here's my reality: I managed to strategize myself right out of a place to live, a job and virtually everything else I own except for the clothes on my back."

My surprise must have shown on my face because she continues with a smirk. "Yeah, I'm a college graduate now I can make plans without a single thought to contingencies. Aren't I just flippin' brilliant? I don't have a place to live, I don't have a job, I don't have a way to get to my medical appointments. I recently turned twenty-eight — and now I've got an appointment with the Grim Reaper and there isn't a single soul in my life left to care. If that isn't a pathetically sad commentary on my life, I don't know what is."

"Okay, I tend to be a little analytical about these problems, call it an occupational hazard. Let's work this through backwards — you know like an equation."

"I'm a math teacher," she responds skeptically. "That makes me abundantly qualified to tell you there's no way to solve my life like an equation."

I smile at her. "As much as I highly respect brilliant women, just humor me here."

"You do know you wouldn't work the equation backwards?" she asks with a raised eyebrow.

I chuckle lightly. "Yes, I think I remember the basics. I might make my living with words, but I still remember rudimentary facts about pre-algebra," I reply. "Just for the sake of argument—"

"Oh, good gravy, I should've remembered you were one of those fancy lawyer types before I started this conversation —" Shelby grumbles under her breath.

"I did try to warn you — I come with built-in occupational hazards."

Shelby pops another French fry in her mouth as she leans back in the wrought iron chair and crosses her arms and waits for me to speak. "I've got to hear how you think math is going to save me from skin cancer," she challenges.

"I don't know if math is going to do any of that. However, breaking your problem down into small pieces might make it easier to handle. For example, you said that you don't have anybody in your life who cares about you. I happen to know you're wrong. Jade and Rogue are very concerned about you. Come to think of it, so am I. By my count, that makes at least three of us and I bet by the response you got a few weeks ago at the shop there are probably several more people who care about you. That number doesn't even include the people who you went to school with, the people who live near you, or the people you've worked with —"

"Mark, what kind of person you do think I am?" Shelby exclaims shaking her head in disbelief. "I can't take advantage of people like that. I don't know these people. I wandered into Ink'd Deep a few weeks ago to get a tattoo. These people don't know me from Adam. They certainly don't owe me anything,"

"What if they want to help?" I argue.

"Why would they want to?" she counters. "People just aren't that nice — unless they want something."

"What if they were?" .

Shelby grows quiet for a moment. "I don't know if I could trust that."

"Shelby, I know you don't know me very well, but I have reason to believe we have many connections between our souls. Can you find it in yourself to trust me?"

I inwardly cringe as the words come out of my mouth, I don't know what I'm actually saying, but it doesn't stop me. I watch as an expression of disbelief crosses her face and then something akin to resignation follows.

Finally, she's slowly nods. "I don't know why I'm even saying this, but I think I can trust you."

CHAPTER THREE

SHELBY

I'M STILL NOT SURE what happened to me that night. One moment I was having an existential meltdown next to a couple of smelly dumpsters, and the next minute my life was being systematically put back together by the singularly best-looking man I have ever seen in my entire life. He didn't even seem to notice I was a sniveling mess of snot and tears. How he could've missed that I was a wreck, I'm not exactly sure. In retrospect, I'm just glad he didn't make a big deal out of it.

It was the most surreal thing I've ever seen in my whole life. I went inside Ink'd Deep to wash my hands and by the time I was done, it appeared several people had a committee meeting about me and essentially sorted out my entire life. Some people might have taken exception to such an intrusive level of planning — but at this point, everything is out of my control. I'm grateful anyone actually cared enough to step up and do something to help me.

Apparently, Jade's parents want to travel and they would like someone to live on their property. They're willing to let me live there in exchange for me keeping an eye on their pets and plants while they're gone. It seemed almost too good to be true — there must be a catch. When I asked Jade about it, she softly smiled. "I went through a dark stage as a teenager. The posters are pretty creepy, you'll probably have to redecorate my room."

If that weren't enough, Jade's mom, Diamond, told me about several volunteer opportunities at the library where I could use my teaching degree. When I expressed concerns about my ability to work consistently because of the cancer, Diamond simply hugged me and said they would work around whatever schedule I was able to work. It's not the job I wanted, and it's not a paid opportunity, but it's better than moping around at home watching game shows and soap operas. For the first time since I got my diagnosis, I have hope. I might have some semblance of normalcy in my everyday life after all.

I look across the car at Mark as he weaves his way through traffic. "You didn't really have to do this, I could've caught the bus or something. I thought you had a trial today."

"I did, but the docket got rearranged because the other side is bringing in an expert witness and they weren't available."

"What happens when I have an appointment and your schedule doesn't get conveniently rearranged?" I challenge.

"I'll figure something out," Mark answers with a shrug. "I have to do it all the time with Ketki. It comes with the territory of being a single dad."

"But … Mark … *argh*," I sputter with frustration. "I'm not your kid. I'm some random stranger you literally picked up off the ground, you don't have to do all this for me."

"Shelby, I can't explain it, but I need to be here. Since the first time I saw you at Ink'd, I knew you'd be in my life."

I curl away from him and face toward the door. His words frighten me — they are too much like the words Josiah Frachett used to lure my parents away from reality. I know that too many sweet words, charm and charisma can cost lives. I might be deathly ill, but I'm not stupid enough to fall into his trap. I won't be gullible like my parents; I've come too far. I've worked too hard. I *cannot* be like the little girl I once was.

Just then, the car ahead of us abruptly stops. Mark throws his arm out to shield me from the dashboard. It's a sweet gesture but, completely unnecessary. I am a compulsive seatbelt wearer. I spent too many years being bounced around in the back of a bus to forgo the luxury of being secure in my seat.

Mark takes a good look at me after we are stopped in traffic. "What's wrong? You're extremely pale — are you feeling ill?" His voice is laced with concern.

It's a funny thing about living on the edge of not knowing whether you're close to dying. You get a little braver and tend to say the things you might not otherwise say.

I blow my bangs out of my eyes. "I guess you can say an unhappy trip down memory lane caught up with me for a second."

"What do you mean?"

"I'd tell you, but I think we're probably almost to the

hospital and it will take more time than we have."

Mark sits up a little taller in the driver's seat and cranes his neck. He frowns. "I hate to break it to you, but I think we're going to be here for a bit."

"Oh no, what about my appointment?" I fret, as I nervously shake my Diet Mountain Dew. The ice melted long ago. Now I'm just fidgeting.

"As backed up as the freeway is, I suspect the personnel at the hospital already knows. You can call them and let them know — just to make sure."

"I think I'll do that," I offer. Unfortunately, when I try to call the doctor's office, I hear nothing but a busy signal.

Mark sees my frustration. He takes my drink from me and makes a motion for me to hand him my phone. "Relax, no one is going anywhere fast. I think we'll be here for a while. They will understand; if you're late, chances are, some doctors will be late too. I wouldn't worry about it; If you can't get through, you can't get through."

"The last thing I can afford to do right now is pick up charges for an appointment I don't attend."

"Look at this place. It's like a parking lot. If the hospital tries to bill you, perhaps a letter from Hunters Crossing will set them straight. It's likely dozens and dozens of people won't be able to make their appointments. You won't be alone. If I had to guess, I would say a fair amount of staff won't be there either."

I run my hands through my hair and take a sip of my drink before I turn toward him and try again to explain, "See, that's just it Mark. You can't fix this with poetic, charming, powerful, preachy words. This is *cancer*. Today, I take one more step toward figuring out whether this crap is going to kill me. Do you get that? *Kill me*. As in dead, d-e-a-d, dead. You can't sweet talk my cells into behaving. The damage is done. All those idiotic trips to the tanning beds and the time I spent baking myself on the beach — don't you think I feel stupid now? All I wanted to do was fit in as a teenager and now there's a good chance I'll die for my choices."

"Shelby, how many opinions have you gotten, does this guy even know what he's doing? Have you consulted the top expert in the field? You can't know anything for sure yet. Maybe he's a quack. You have to think positive about this. I know Jade's mom has worn through a set of rosary beads praying for you."

"Sorry to break it to you, Counselor, but for me the jury is still out whether I believe in church or in prayer and all that jazz. All I've seen it do is create death and destruction. If other people want to believe in all that stuff, more power to them. I'm not sure it's all for me."

It's clear Mark isn't prepared for the tone of anger in my voice. His eyes are wide and he just blinks as he absorbs the pain and vitriol I've been storing up for days.

I'm on too much of a roll to stop now. "As far as whether I believe the doctors about the diagnosis; just look at me compared to you. Do you see what I see? I am a walking poster child for risk factors for skin cancer, from my light hair and eyes to my skin, which is *several* shades paler than yours. When I was younger, I never used sunscreen. My parents didn't believe in it. They thought it blocked the vitamins from the sun and when I became a teenager, I actually thought getting a ritualistic burn at the beginning of every summer was a good thing because it would encourage me to tan later. In high school, my friends and I would use baby oil to increase the chances of burning ourselves." My speech trails off as I run out of steam.

"I'll admit your risk factors don't sound ideal, but you don't know the whole picture yet. Cancer treatment has come a long way in recent years," Mark argues. "You're young and otherwise healthy, right?"

I groan. "Thanks for reminding me. I turned twenty-eight last week. I'm not even thirty years old yet and I might have to plan my own funeral. Doesn't that just suck monkey balls?"

"Oh, look at you … still in your twenties. I feel positively ancient. I hit thirty-five a couple months ago. Everybody in my office wants to throw me an over-the-hill party," he teases, before growing serious. "Actually, it does really suck. Cancer is terrible, regardless of how old you are. I'm sorry you're even having to deal with this. We should be having a huge graduation party for you, not heading to the doctor."

I blush. "Would you believe that the little impromptu celebration at Ink'd Deep was the closest thing I've ever had to a party?"

Mark's eyebrows raise in surprise. "Really? You didn't even have parties as a kid? Not even Chuck E. Cheese?"

I shake my head. "No, my parents had some rather unconventional beliefs. At first, I think it was just a matter of poverty, but then, as their belief-paradigm began to shift, more and more things you'd normally associate with childhood began to fall away."

"What do you mean?" Mark moves the car forward a few feet before he has to stop again.

"I have vague memories of starting out in a relatively normal household, but it didn't stay that way for long. I know we used to walk my big sister to school when my mom was pregnant with my little brother. I remember running home from school and my mom trying to cover her head with a newspaper."

"It's funny what we remember from our childhood, isn't it?"

I nod. "Then something happened and my dad stopped working. He bought an old school bus and we started moving from town to town in the bus. My dad was a pretty good handyman. He used to get jobs here and there helping to remodel people's homes. Something occurred during Owen's birth and my brother seemed to struggle from the start."

"Wow! Must've been tough," Mark comments with sympathy in his voice.

"I was pretty little, I didn't know what was happening, really. I just knew that Owen was more like one of my play dolls than a real baby. In the beginning, he didn't even cry much. Suddenly, my parents went on this epic quest to fix Owen. My dad stopped working altogether and we traveled from church to church looking for prayer services and revival meetings. Sometimes my sister Savannah and I would have to walk around the town asking people for things to eat. Of course, back then I was so little, I thought it was like a game of hide and seek. I wasn't old enough to understand the social implications of what I was doing, but Savannah — she's five years older than I am — understood we were basically panhandling and she was never okay with it."

"Where is your family now?" Mark pulls up into the parking garage.

"I honestly don't know. I haven't heard from my parents in years, and it seems like my sister dropped off the face of the planet." My voice drops to a whisper as I add, "Owen is buried somewhere in the mountains of West Virginia. They left him far behind because we didn't have a permanent home."

"What do you mean? You just graduated from college — weren't they there? Shelby, what happened to your brother?"

I look around at our surroundings and calculate the amount of time we have until we reach the door. There really is no way to put my life story into a nutshell, but the look of intense curiosity on Mark's face tells me he won't let this go anytime soon.

"You've probably seen people like this on the news — you may have even seen my parents — I don't know. A lot of people don't even remember how crazy it was back during Y2K, but my parents went absolutely nuts. They were going from place to place trying to find someone to fix Owen. Eventually they settled for this charismatic preacher — a cult leader, really — named Josiah Frachett. He was exotic with a foreign accent. He could speak several languages — or at least pretend to with enough bravado to make everyone believe him. He was suave and debonair and he could recite the Bible with astounding ease; he made it sound like lines of poetry."

"Your parents didn't know about Jim Jones or Heaven's Gate?" Mark asks incredulously.

"I honestly don't know what they knew back then. Reverend Josiah kept members of the congregation from talking to outsiders … and sometimes each other. The longer my family followed The Righteous Universe Calling, the more bizarre the ministry became. He taught them to be afraid of all books, magazines and television — especially the news. All medical intervention from the outside was forbidden because Reverend Josiah began prophesying about the end of the world by the year 2000 and that in the kingdom of God, He wanted our bodies unsullied by the hands of mankind."

Mark visibly winces as he softly inquires, "Your brother?"

"I'm not exactly sure. Savannah had the most responsibility for him, but he was always very weak. It could've been a seizure, an allergic reaction or maybe even an infection. I think if he would've had proper medical help, he might have lived. Anyway, it was the beginning of the end of our family. After Owen died, my family could no longer hide from the authorities and the police came in and took me away. Apparently, Savannah was old enough to make her own decision. To this day, I don't know what she decided. My parents elected to stay with the Righteous Universe Calling. I wasn't even allowed to go to Owen's funeral. Suddenly, I was alone in the world."

Mark shakes his head in disbelief. "That's terrible. No child should be left alone in the world because of a parent's poor decisions. I'm sorry you lost your brother. It must've been awful."

"It was really hard on Savannah and me. My parents had pretty much left the raising of Owen up to us after they got involved with Reverend Josiah. We felt really guilty because he died, but we didn't have the tools to save him because we weren't going to school and we couldn't keep him safe."

"I'm surprised your parents weren't criminally charged for negligent manslaughter in the death of your brother," Mark declares angrily.

"Perhaps with today's social media, more would've been done, but you have to remember this happened sixteen years ago. There wasn't any public pressure to pursue it. The authorities chalked it up to a religious decision and once they decided I was safe and my sister was old enough to fend for herself. There was no motivation to take things further. After my parents disappeared back into the streets with Reverend Josiah — the authorities let the matter drop," I explain with a shrug.

"Aren't you angry that there was no justice for your brother? It hardly seems fair." As I watched the passion flare in his eyes, I can see why he's probably such an effective attorney. I can almost see legal arguments forming in his mind as he asks me questions. It's fascinating to see how quickly he's jumped to my defense.

I sigh. "I'm finding very little seems fair in my life."

When we finally made it to the hospital and Mark stops to wait for the gate to go up at the parking lot. He pulls his sporty little car into a spot and throws it into Park. He walks around the car and opens the door for me. When someone's car alarm goes off in the parking garage and scares me, he puts his arm around my shoulder and soothes, "*Immokalee*, easy I've got you. It was just a loud car horn."

Mary Crawford

Given my notorious love of freedom, his arm should feel more like a trap and less like a warm embrace. Yet, as I snuggle closer to his side, I'm in no hurry to leave the cocoon of his rock-solid presence.

CHAPTER FOUR

MARK

I PLAYED A LITTLE football in high school. As an attorney and a single dad, I consider myself to be pretty tough, but after Shelby's visit with the plastic surgeon, I realize I've got no idea what it means to be tough. Shelby was planning to do this by herself, I can't even fathom her grit and determination. Had the medical office not put the brakes on her plan, she was planning to drive herself to her appointment — or more precisely — she was planning to ride her bicycle. As I watch her restlessly sleeping in the passenger seat, I am glad I was my usual insistent self. Sometimes, pushy works.

I'd like her to see a different specialist. I am not thrilled with the bedside manner of this particular doctor. She seemed to gloss over Shelby's questions and went forward with her plan of action even though Shelby still had doubts. Before Shelby could even process what was being said, this doctor already had the laser out and was removing layers of skin and announcing her plans for other areas which still need to be treated. She did this with a stunning level of casualness. It's as if she was telling Shelby to buy potato chips and milk. Without pattern or explanation she scraped a few areas, other areas she froze, while she zapped others with a laser tool. All the while talking with great glee about the one spot on Shelby's back she could excavate as if it was a complicated road construction project.

Rather than take the time to reassure Shelby and explain the surgery's benefits, she was talking about how fun it would be for her to have to restructure her skin flap from another part of Shelby's leg. She took no time to explain why some of Shelby's cancer was more serious than others or how she made the call between one form of treatment and another. Before it was all said and done, I had lost track of the number of places this so-called specialist cut, froze or burned on Shelby's skin. She was talking so quickly even I lost track of what was going on. By the end, Shelby was woozy and nauseous. She was shaking from head to toe and her teeth were chattering so hard that she could not speak. I had to borrow a wheelchair to escort her out to my car. If I had known this visit would be so intrusive, I would have helped her make arrangements to be treated at a proper surgical center instead of a doctor's office.

Shelby whimpers in pain and shifts in her seat. The blanket I threw over her slides down. I pull it back up over her shoulder. For once, I am grateful for the amount of preparation my life requires me to have. I have at least two blankets with me at all times and often times I have many more. At the doctor's insistence, Shelby is staying the night in my guest room. It's one of the few things the doctor suggested I actually support.

As I'm driving home, I'm trying to remember the state of the spare room. The last time I checked it, Ketki was using it to house her extensive feather and pebble collection. She had the whole bed covered with feathers

— arranged by size and color matched with a corresponding pebble whose criteria only makes sense to her. She is meticulous and obsessive about her collection. She tends to move it around though, so hopefully it has changed location since the last time I saw it. Fortunately, my sister, Leotie, is watching Ketki at the moment, so at least that's one less worry.

Worried. It seems to be my perpetual state of being since this beautiful sprite wandered into my life. I can't seem to help myself. When I'm with her, I worry about what kind of impression I'm making and if I'm being helpful enough or if I'm being overbearing. If I'm not with Shelby, I wonder if she's happy, lonely or stressed. At what point in my life did I become such a sentimental sap?

I pull the car into the carport, taking care to avoid Ketki's bike. Sometimes, I think she purposefully leaves it out for me to run over. I shake my head and laugh at the thought. My girl is not big on fresh air and exercise. She would much rather play computer games and read obscure library books about archaic topics. The car slows to a stop and Shelby moans as the seatbelt rubs against one of the bandages on her collarbone. She's curled into a tight ball like a pill bug. That's no easy feat in my small bucket seats.

I reach out to gently stroke Shelby's cheek in an effort to wake her up, but she doesn't stir. When I call her name, her eyelashes flicker briefly, but her eyes do not open. It's getting humid in my car, so I make the decision to carry her inside. As I walk around the car and scoop her up in my arms, she strains to position her cheek more comfortably on my chest. The first thing I noticed is how comfortably Shelby fits in my arms. She settles closer and lets out a small sigh. I weave my way through the house, leaving as many lights off as possible so I don't disturb Shelby. When I check the guest room, I am dismayed to discover that Ketki has completely taken it over with her display of found objects. Quickly reversing course, I move Shelby to the master bedroom and place her in the middle of my bed. I guess it was a lucky break that Ketki spilled her chocolate milk on my bed this morning and I changed all of my sheets and blankets. I'll just make up the guest room for myself.

After I get Shelby suitably tucked in and propped up with pillows, I set out to clear out the guest room by placing all of Ketki's treasures on a piece of presentation board that I had left over from my last trial. If I had been thinking ahead, I would've provided this to Ketki before so her display could have been portable to start with. I apply the Post-it note glue I use to make temporary traditional, old-school courtroom displays. Most of the stuff I do in court is done on a computer. Now and then, I have physical demonstrations Which I have to manipulate. This temporary glue is useful and it's handy for Ketki's many collections.

I'm trying to have a level of precision which will meet my daughter's exacting standards as I transfer her precious objects to the new surface. She knows each and every feather and stone by heart — if I disturb the order of things, she will be devastated. Just as I'm about to position the last row of feathers on the board, I lean too hard on the bed and the pebbles roll toward the middle of the bed. The bottom drops out of my stomach. Ketki has an intricate sorting system for her pebbles. They all appear similar to me; but to her, they match specific feathers. I don't know if I'll be able to put it back together correctly.

I have to crawl up onto the bed to make sure I've missed none of the smaller stones. I'm completely caught off guard by a low chuckle and wolf whistle coming from the doorway. I look back over my shoulder and catch Shelby ogling my backside.

I raise an eyebrow in question. "It is not like I'm not grateful or anything — and I'll be especially thankful if I get these kind of views — but if the room I'm in is the guest room, I'm seriously outclassed here. You didn't tell me you were planning to give up your bedroom for me. That's too much," she protests.

I gesture at my impromptu craft project and try to explain, "My daughter, Ketki, has autism and she sometimes uses this room to store her collection. She is very choosy about how it's organized. She had it on the bed and I was trying to move it without disturbing it. I was doing well until the last little bit, but I'm afraid I messed it up. I am going to be voted World's Worst Dad unless I can figure out her system." I show her the collection of pebbles in my hand.

Shelby quietly walks over to the little display board I've started and studies it carefully. She reaches toward my hand. "You mind? I think I see a pattern."

"You do?" I blurt, unable to disguise my astonishment. "Ketki's been mining feathers, stones and shells almost since she was a baby and I've never determined a rhyme or reason to her methods." I hand Shelby the remaining stones and watch as she efficiently sorts them and places them next to their corresponding feather.

Shelby smiles shyly. "I spent a lot of time by myself as a kid, I used to make up all sorts of games in my head. I often see patterns and designs where other people don't.

I think that's what makes me good at math."

I shake my head in amazement. "How in the world did you do it? I don't want to seem stupid, but I have no idea. I've long ago accepted that Ketki is far brighter than me in many ways, so this isn't a newsflash, but I am curious —"

Shelby gives me a small nod. "Now, of course — this is Ketki's system and I could always be wrong — but from what I see, she first identified all the stones which had spots in them like the spots in the feathers and she sorted them by the numbers from highest to lowest and then when she ran out of numbers, she started sorting by each predominant color."

I'm sure the shock on my face makes me look like an exaggerated cartoon character, but I can't contain my utter amazement. Her conclusion isn't unfamiliar because it sounds exactly like Ketki. My daughter has been known to take the ingredients out of minestrone soup and sort it before she eats it. My surprise comes not only from the fact that Shelby could figure it out so quickly, but completely without judgment.

"Now that you say it, it makes perfect sense, but I swear I have seen her sort those things thousands of times, and never came up with a pattern." My face heats with shame.

Shelby *tsks* me like the teacher that she is. "Mark, it's not an obvious pattern. If your brain doesn't think in an offbeat sort of way like mine does, it wouldn't have occurred to you. It's okay, everybody's brain works differently. Does your wife's brain work more like Ketki's brain or more like yours?"

I pull Shelby toward me until she's sitting on the bed

at my side. "Shelby, there's no easy way to talk about this, so I'll just tell you."

I watch as Shelby visibly braces herself. She swallows hard and curls her body over until she's a small shadow of her confident self. I can't figure out what she's doing, but she looks scared. "Shelby, this has nothing to do with you and everything to do with Tayanita, my ex-wife and Ketki's mom."

"Are you sure? I've been out of commission and relying on you a lot. You've been very generous. Perhaps I've been taking advantage of your generosity."

"Shelby, unless you're planning to say vile things and storm out because you can't deal with my daughter's disabilities like she did, you don't have anything to worry about," I inform her grimly.

I can read every emotion which flits across Shelby's face as she processes what I said. She opens and closes her mouth several times before she finally regains the power of speech.

"Please tell me you're kidding," Shelby pleads. "That's a rotten reason to decide not to be a mom. I've seen some pretty poor parenting decisions — but hers ranks right up there."

"I don't know if Tayanita fully understands the ramifications of her choices. Growing up, she was the oldest sibling in charge of all of her brothers and sisters. Ketki's birth was unplanned. We had been taking steps to prevent pregnancy, but they failed. Tayanita was not thrilled to be pregnant in the first place and then when it became clear something was not exactly right with Ketki, it was the very last straw. It was simply more than Tayanita could take. Rather than make us all unhappy, she took off."

"You make it sound like she had onion rings instead of French fries," Shelby responds with disbelief. "Didn't her decision disrupt your whole life?"

"Absolutely. I was studying for the bar exam and trying to arrange emergency daycare for Ketki. It was crazy. Back in those days, I didn't know what was wrong, we just knew something was. I mean, I had a feeling I knew what it was, because her symptoms were pretty typical. The hand-flapping was a pretty good giveaway. Even so, I had to take her to a series of doctors, therapists, speech therapists, psychologists and everyone in between. This seemed to go on for months and months, but eventually we figured out a routine. My family was a big help — they still are. That's where Ketki is right now. My sister is watching her for me. Ketki's cousin is having a slumber party for her birthday and invited her to come."

"Aren't you ticked off at your wife? I would be. I don't know if I could forgive something like that," Shelby covers her mouth in shock. "Oh, I'm so sorry … that probably wasn't appropriate for me to say."

I shrug. "I don't know. You're entitled to your opinion. Some days, I ask myself the same questions —"

Chapter Five

Shelby

THIS IS THE BEST nap I've had in quite a while — or it was until I feel my eye being pried open by small fingers. Startled, I open my eyes and come face-to-face with a somber little girl with long black hair wearing a Wonder Woman T-shirt and bright red shorts. She is intently studying me, but she never looks me directly in the eye. Finally, she mumbles softly, "You're in my daddy's bed. Are you my new mom? How come your hair is white? Did you curl it with a curling iron? How come you're not wearing pajamas? Why do you have Band-Aids all over?"

"That's a lot of questions. Do I get to pick and choose which order I answer them in?" I tease. "Hi, my name is Shelby. I'm your dad's friend. He is letting me borrow his bed because I wasn't feeling so great after I went to the doctor this morning. I have bad cells growing in my skin and the doctor took a few off today, which is why I have all these silly Band-Aids. Unfortunately, the doctor didn't have any Wonder Woman bandages. That would've been cool but I'm stuck with the regular kind."

I tap my chin in thought. "Let's see — did I miss anything?"

Ketki rolls up on her toes and back onto her heels several times. "My friend Kristi got a new mommy after there was a new lady in her daddy's bed. So are you my mom now?"

I feel myself blush. Well, this is interesting … Why do I feel like I need to do a walk of shame when I haven't done anything inappropriate? I'll have to answer this question very carefully.

I see the potential for this conversation to get off track quite easily. I'm not entirely sure if Mark wanted me to meet his daughter. We never even talked about it. I know some parents are reluctant to let their children know they even have a social life. Either way, I'm sure he's not ready for Ketki to be jumping to these kinds of conclusions. For now, I elect to go for a straightforward and simple answer.

"Your dad was worried about me after my surgery because I don't have any family around. He offered to take care of me for a couple days until I feel stronger."

"If you need a toothbrush, the dentist gave me one. I don't like pink," she offers. "Girls don't have to like pink. Dad said."

"I agree. I think the color thing is silly. I will take you up on the toothbrush thing. I was in a hurry this morning and I forgot mine. Can you do me a favor and show me where everything is? I'm a little lost in this big house."

For a moment, Ketki stands stock still in the middle of the room. I hold my breath as she makes her decision. Finally, she tilts her head toward the door. "Okay."

The little imp doesn't give me time to get myself together before she takes off. I scramble to get out of bed and follow her. Fortunately, she hasn't traveled far. I find her in front of an open medicine cupboard. She is jumping up and down trying to snag a hot pink toothbrush off of one of the top shelves. "I'm not Dad," she explains simply. I notice she is rhythmically moving her left hand more than she was before. If she's like the students I've worked with before, it probably means she's feeling overwhelmed.

I step toward the sink and reach over her head and grab the toothbrush. "I completely understand. I'm not a lot taller than you are. I get totally frustrated when I can't reach something. Thank you for letting me have this. Where to next?" I ask, as she leads us out of the bathroom.

At the bottom of the stairs, Ketki comes to a halt. She turns toward me, but looks past my head as she asks, "You play video games?"

I roll my shoulder casually and nod. "It depends. I'm not exactly a noob, but I'm not any sort of pro either."

"Good." She motions for me to follow her. We walk down the hall and at the end Ketki opens the double wooden doors to what presumably is the den. In my mind, I expected it to be a stereotypical library like you see in all those commercials for law offices. I couldn't have been more wrong. This room is something right out of a gamer's fantasy. I am speechless for several moments as I stand in the middle of the room and take it all in. There are big monitors and little monitors, new systems and old and every input device you can imagine. I walk over to a large gaming chair with speakers in the head rest and sit down. "This is positively decadent; be honest with me, who plays more video games? You or your dad?"

Ketki looks at me blankly as if what I asked is the most ridiculous question in the world. "I do. My school gets out earlier than Dad's work. Plus, he sometimes brings work home on the weekend, or he has to travel far away to do a trial."

I sigh dramatically. "I'm sorry. Sometimes being a grown-up is a drag. I'm sure your dad wishes he had more time to play video games. This is the coolest game room I have ever seen. I would be playing in here all the time."

Ketki's shoulders slump. "I like it too, but not everybody does."

"What do you mean?"

"People don't like me much. They won't even come for a birthday party. I even told them I had a bunch of new games. Nobody came, not even Kristi."

"That's a royal bummer. It kinda sucks for them too. They missed out on a chance to be friends with somebody cool. Your hangout place is pretty awesome. I guess they won't know that now."

Ketki stares down at the ground. "How do you know?"

"How do I know what?" I ask to clarify.

"How do you know I'm cool? You just met me. Most people don't stick around long — even my mom left once she got to know me, so I must not be so cool."

"Ketki, I can look around this room and see you have an appreciation for gaming history. You understand new technology too. I see the huge puzzle hanging on the wall. I know it must've been difficult. I bet it took lots of patience. Not everybody could do something so complicated. I see books on the bookshelf about Isaac

Newton and Pythagoras. I'm willing to bet those are your books and not your dad's. From one smart chick to another, I think it totally rocks that you like mathematics. Sometimes people make decisions which don't make any sense. It can be hard to understand from the outside. I don't know your mom and I don't know why she had to make her choices, but I doubt it was because she doesn't like you."

"It seems that way," mumbles Ketki.

I want to collect Ketki in a giant bear hug, but her body language is throwing up all sorts of caution signs so I shrug. "I know — but sometimes things aren't always what they seem."

Rogue is treating me to a day of consignment store shopping. I had no idea she'd have credit at almost every store we shopped at. What's more, she's insisting that I use her credit to rebuild my wardrobe. By the time we stop for lunch, my stress level is at an all-time high. I had no idea she meant to completely deck me out from head to toe. I'm merely working at the library to build experience for my resume. Don't tell that to Little-Miss-Headhunter over here. She's too busy dressing me for a Fortune 500 Company.

After we have taken a few bites of our sandwiches, Rogue casually asks, "How is life at Mister-Tall-Dark-and-Handsome's?"

I take a long drink of my Diet Mountain Dew. "I forgot to tell you; I'm not there anymore. I went back to Jett and Diamond's place."

Rogue's mouth opens in shock. "I thought he was inventing new ways to spoil you."

I nervously fiddle with my straw. "I can't complain about the way he's treated me, that's for sure. He made me breakfast in bed every single day. I didn't really need him to do that, especially after the first day. I was a little stiff, sore and exhausted, but I didn't need such an extreme level of pampering. I could've curled up on my own couch with a box of Wheat-Thins, a can of Cheez-Whiz and a liter of Dew and I would've gotten along just fine."

"I'm not known for being the food police, but even I know that stuff will kill you," Rogue warns.

I level an exasperated stare at Rogue as I remind her, "Newsflash: a little orange food coloring is the least of my worries right now. I'm in very real danger of other things killing me first — you know, things like … I dunno … pesky little cancer cells."

Rogue shrugs. "All I'm saying is that there's no need to be reckless while they're treating your skin cancer — it would be a bummer to fix all the skin cancer only to find out you destroyed your health binging on junk food, right?"

"You're as big a party-pooper as Ketki. She recites all the calories and fat for everything I put in my mouth. Do you know how hard it is to justify a Krispy Kreme when you know exactly how many calories it has in it? Oh … and forget about Monte Cristo sandwiches altogether. There aren't enough excuses on the planet for those."

Rogue takes a sip of her Pepsi. "How do you get along with Mark's little girl? Tristan and I are talking about having kids. Tristan is leaning toward adoption because of what happened with his sister and nephew."

I slump back against my chair in defeat as I confess the difficult truth. "I adore Ketki and I'm sure she thinks I'm related to one of the inventors of YouTube or something. She follows my every move like it's a new computer code."

Rogue shoots me an amused grin as she responds, "So why do you look like Marcus does when someone takes his Red Bull? It's better than her hating your guts. I did a modeling gig with somebody whose stepdaughter absolutely loathed her. It was pretty ugly. She actually came to work with a bite mark on her face."

"That's extreme. Still, I wonder if it might be better if Ketki didn't like me quite so much. We've been playing video games for two days straight. She's an amazing kid. Super shy at first, but incredibly smart. She kicks my butt at video games."

"She does?" Rogue asks, perking up with interest. "Tristan is always looking for talented people to test his new stuff." As she cleans our garbage off of the table, she stops and asks me, "Wait! Why would Ketki be better off if she didn't like you? I'm confused … I thought you guys hit it off."

Before I can stop it, I let out a growl of frustration. "Rogue, don't you get it? I hate my life. You shouldn't even be in my life. No one should be in my life right now — none of you guys from Ink'd, not Mark and especially not Ketki. You all don't deserve what might happen. You have been incredible to me — *Good Lord*, I showed up on your doorstep like an abandoned kitten and you all took me on like the town project and this stupid cancer might take me away before I even have time to properly thank you all. I can't do that to Ketki. She already struggles to make friends, I can't duck into her life and then die. She would be devastated."

Rogue comes over and squats next to me as she grabs a hold of my hands. "You're right. You are absolutely right. It would devastate all of us. It would be especially crushing for a little girl who idolizes you. Here's the deal: you're already in our lives. We already like you. There is no going back. Here's the other piece of news you need to focus on — there is a better than 90% chance you'll come out of this okay. You might be a little scarred and not quite so perfect, but you'll be here. You won't get rid of us so easily. We are a pesky bunch."

My eyes instantly fill up with tears and my voice becomes shaky. "Ninety percent, huh? Are you sure? The doctor I met with sounded out-and-out dire. She told me to get my affairs in order — as if I had anybody around to care. I'd hate to get my hopes up for nothing. My upbringing was a little weird, I don't know who to believe anymore."

"You remember meeting Tristan and Isaac when Delaney Jane was giving you your tattoo?"

"That's your *husband?*" I ask, my eyes wide with shock. "I'm sorry; I've just never seen anybody be so particular about where a cash register goes. Who was the guy arguing with him?"

"Would you believe that's my dad?" Rogue answers with an eye roll. "It's safe to say both those guys sweat the small details. When I told Tristan about you, we did some in-depth research and found out the facts because we were worried. You can take Tristan's sources to the bank. If you need them to, they could probably find you the researchers who performed the studies to explain them to you. Padre-Pop and Tristan work in mysterious ways. I have learned never to underestimate them."

I can't hold it in any longer and I start to cry. Alarmed, Rogue puts her arms around me and quietly absorbs my fear and pain.

As I pull away, she softly whispers, "I'm sorry, Shelby. I wish I could wave a magic wand and make it all go away."

"As odd as this sounds, I don't know if I'd wish the same," I confess. "Before I had the ugly C word in my life, I was alone with no one and now you all have become like the family I haven't had in decades. No one ever wishes to get cancer, but if gaining you was the trade I had to make, it almost makes it worthwhile."

Rogue gives me a brief hug and teasingly remarks, "I don't know, you've got some tough times ahead of you and we can be a pretty strange group. You might decide we're not worth the bargain."

CHAPTER SIX

MARK

"YOU SUCK AT THIS," Ketki announces for about the fifteenth time tonight. "Why can't you be more like Shelby? It was more fun when she was here." Again, my daughter has a flair for stating the obvious.

"I'm sorry, Ketki. I'm a little distracted tonight, I've got a big meeting at work tomorrow and my brain is elsewhere. Why don't you invite some friends over this weekend and have a slumber party or something?"

"D-a-a-a-d, do you even know anything about my friends?" Ketki challenges, drawing my name out into several syllables.

"Do they go to school?"

Ketki pauses and then nods carefully.

"Are they as nice as you?" I tease.

Ketki grins and nods enthusiastically.

"If they've been here before, just invite them back. I've got plenty of food. You guys can rent movies and make popcorn or do the girl thing and do each other's hair and all that jazz. Maybe your Aunt Leotie can come over."

My daughter's face changes, and as she stands up to walk away, she murmurs under her breath, "It's like you don't even *know* me."

Ketki's words haunt me for the rest of the evening. How well do I know my daughter? I know what medications she's on. I know what she's allergic to. I know what makes it difficult for her to sleep. I know what will cause her to have a meltdown in the middle of a store. I know what her educational plan is for the school year. I know what therapies she's had to cope with her autism. I know the diagnosis codes we put on her insurance paperwork. I know the behavioral therapies we tried; I know which ones have been epic failures and which ones have shown promise. I know which doctors in the area are total quacks. I know what diet allegedly helps her and which foods should be avoided.

Even so, her words come back to me like a bad jury verdict. I play them over and over in my mind. How much do I *really* know about her? Presumably, I don't know her as well as Shelby does. I've never seen my daughter as happy as she was when Shelby was here. It was simply astonishing to see. There didn't seem to be any artifice or stiffness surrounding it.

Shelby found one of my old sweatshirts. It was beat up and threadbare, but Shelby didn't seem to mind, she just put it on and rolled up the sleeves. She borrowed one of my baseball caps from the Florida Bar and wore it backwards. Of course, Ketki was keen on copying her style. She too wore an oversized Old Navy sweatshirt and a Pokémon baseball cap also donned backwards. Every time I saw the two of them, they seemed to be in the throes of an epic video game battle.

As I listened closely, I realized Shelby was waiting for Ketki to teach her how to play each game. It was clear from watching Shelby handle the controls to the games she needed no such instruction. Unlike many of Ketki's previous opponents, Shelby seemed to take it in stride when my daughter completely annihilated her and she seemed genuinely interested in Ketki's almost obsessive knowledge of Easter eggs, lag times, and known programming glitches in each game.

I freely admit that when Ketki talks about the minutia of each individual video game, my eyes glaze over despite my best intentions — but much to my surprise, Shelby appeared to be genuinely interested in everything Ketki had to say. It makes me curious about what else my daughter shared with Shelby. If I'm honest with myself, it's not only Ketki who was much happier with Shelby around. Even though she was tired and sore, her simple enjoyment of small things was contagious. Her shock and awe over my culinary skills in the kitchen is both baffling and highly amusing.

I do all right in the kitchen. After all, I've been a single dad for about seven years. If I hadn't figured my way around the house quickly, we would have been overrun with dirty laundry and we would've starved to death. Consequently, I have a few general go-to meals and I have learned to do laundry on a regular schedule. If I don't, all heck breaks loose. From what she reported, nothing in Shelby's background prepared her for the idea a man could actually perform routine household tasks. She had just never seen it done, so it was a source of endless fascination for her. She almost seemed horrified by the very thought. It was all I could do to encourage her to sit and rest according to the doctor's instructions.

As soon as Shelby felt stronger, I made a game of my routine chores to make them a family activity and included her. Ketki and I work together in the kitchen all the time, but including a new person in our routine sometimes resulted in some pretty hysterical results. One morning as I was preparing to make pancakes, Shelby, and I reached for the box of pancake mix at the same time and I ended up dumping it all over her head. I expected Shelby to be a little put out with me, but she just ran her fingers through her hair and mumbled something about it being a good treatment for oily hair as she started laughing.

Of course, Ketki immediately wanted to be part of the action because Shelby was having so much fun. Shelby warned her it would be a pain to wash out of her hair, but Ketki wanted to do it anyway, so Shelby took her outside and dumped a bit on her hair too and then they shook the pancake mix through their hair and asked me to take pictures of their strangely ghostlike appearance. After it was all said and done, they looked at each other and announced, "Spa day!" and set off on a whole new adventure. It was the most carefree I have seen Ketki in years. I've gotten so used to Ketki and I being a little self-contained unit that I never stopped to think what she might be missing by not having Tayanita around.

The issues with Ketki's mom are tough. I keep thinking that she'll wake up one day and realize all the things she's missing and remember she still loves me and we'll be the family I always envisioned. I guess I'm the one who should wake up and smell the coffee because she's been gone for better than half a decade now. I don't suppose she'll waltz in through the front door anytime soon.

After I got through the toddler years with Ketki and got her potty trained, we seemed to become an unstoppable team. Until I saw Ketki interacting with Shelby, it never occurred to me she might feel like a piece of our family is missing.

I'm trying to concentrate on reviewing my materials for the board meeting tomorrow, but I can't stop thinking about Shelby. I know my fanciful musings are traveling down some very dangerous paths. Even though my life is a disaster area in the making with so many balls up in the air, I can't even pretend that I'm competently juggling them anymore.

In my mind's eye, I can see adding Shelby to the chaos. In the next breath I have to laugh at my own ego. What's to say she would want to join the circus which is my life? It's not as if I've got everything all figured out and if Shelby needs anything at the moment, it's stability. I'm still working on dealing with getting through the day and coping with Callum's death, the strains of managing the practice and coping with being everything to my daughter. At this point, I don't think I'm prize partner material. Just as I come to that fateful conclusion, one of Ketki's games pops up on the console with loud, garish music and announces Game Over.

I hope it's not prophetic, but I suspect that it might be.

"So you see, if we were able to snag some bigger fish with

deeper pockets, we would be able to fund all this charity work for clients who don't stand a chance of winning and maybe make a profit for a change," Garrett Treadwell smiles, finishing his presentation with a flourish.

I look around the conference room and much to my dismay, everyone in the room appears to be nodding in appreciation. *Crap, he seems to have everyone on board — even all my former classmates from law school. What happened to integrity and doing the practice of law for the greater good? What happened to vanquishing evil no matter what the cost?* Am I the only one who remembers it was supposed to be one of our founding values at Hunters' Crossing? As I watch everyone eat up Garrett's every word, I am resigned to the fact that perhaps I am. Garrett is absorbing all the attention as if he is some sort of A-list movie star.

I want to tell him that this is not an audition for a reality TV show. This is real-life. There are no retakes. Real people's lives are impacted by the decisions we make in this boardroom. This isn't just show and tell. I'm trying hard to separate my personal dislike for his approach to life from the matter at hand. Personally, even though I am his mentor, I think he's a narcissistic pinhead. Even so, I'm not narrow-minded. I do understand that if we don't change the financial climate of the firm, we won't be able to offer health insurance benefits to everyone. I rely on those health insurance benefits to get therapy for Ketki's autism. Talk about your proverbial rock and hard place.

Clearing my throat, I lean forward and address my colleagues, "While I concede Mr. Treadwell has made a few viable points, I hesitate to completely change the complexion of our firm to chase a few dollars in this tight legal market. We have spent a great deal of time and effort to establish a reputation in the legal community. Hunter's Crossing has some standing among our peers. I don't want to throw it away to chase ambulances, as it were. What about the principles we were founded on? We went into business for a specific purpose: are we going to give up our mission just so we can notch up an arbitrary profit margin?"

Garrett openly scoffs at me. "Mark, even you can see that all your principles won't do you any good if this business goes under. Are you living in a fantasyland?"

His utter lack of respect toward me is completely insulting. We're not chowing down on burgers at a corner bar, we are in a formal business meeting which is being recorded for posterity. Instinctively, I sit up straighter in my chair as I level a dark stare at him. "Are you sure the ink on your degree is dry enough for you to be asking those kinds of questions, Mr. Treadwell? I will remind you that the reason you have a job is because my partners and I founded this firm on those principles you're so quick to dismiss. I am well aware of the financial holdings of this firm. At no time did we ever state this firm was anywhere close to folding. The only thing we were discussing was an adjustment to compensation packages. At the moment, I'm wondering if maybe we've gotten a little too generous. Perhaps the associates are feeling a little too entitled."

Anita, the associate who works with Susan, raises her hand and responds, "Mr. Littleson, I hope you understand that I am profoundly honored to work here and grateful for the help you give associates."

"You are a world-class *butt kisser*," Garrett hisses

under his breath toward Anita.

I have to take a moment to collect myself because I'm busy considering options I'd like to say — but probably shouldn't. The kid has no place being in the business of helping people as far as I'm concerned. If I had a magic wand, the snively earwig would sanitize porta-potties for a living. Fortunately for him, I don't run the world. I merely have to operate in it. I simply don't understand how phenomenally brave, smart young men like my brother die and entitled rich losers like this guy live footloose and fancy free — it doesn't make any sense. Before I can even rearrange my chaotic thoughts into some semblance of a coherent response, Susan, the other senior partner present today, walks up behind Garrett.

"Mr. Treadwell, do you have something you would like to share with the rest of us?" she challenges.

He ducks his head. "No ma'am."

Susan narrows her eyes at him as she instructs, "If it was good enough to say to your colleague, you should feel comfortable sharing it with the group. Otherwise, you shouldn't have said it to your colleague. It was incredibly rude. This is a professional office. However, something tells me that perhaps you've forgotten we comport ourselves with decorum in this workplace. This is not the same as watching the playoffs with your buddies in your den."

Garrett blushes as red as I've ever seen him. "Yes, ma'am."

Susan turns to me. "Mr. Littleson, do you have anything to add?"

"I am not blind to the fact that we need to make a

few changes, but I suggest we do a trial run and try to take a couple of new clients in the new areas and see how it changes the complexion of our office. I don't want us to make wholesale changes without understanding what it might do to our structure. I want to dig a little deeper."

"That sounds like a reasonable, balanced approach to me," Susan agrees. "Do you want to focus on Med Mal or product liability?"

"I don't know," I admit. "Let me do some soul-searching."

CHAPTER SEVEN

SHELBY

"MARK, I CAN'T BELIEVE you're here this morning. Doesn't your trial start today?" I look out the front door and I'm barely able to make out the neighborhood in the early morning dawn.

He glances down at himself in his casual outfit. "I suppose you wouldn't believe I was merely out for a run?"

"If it wasn't five in the morning and I didn't live 17 miles from you — oh wait, Ketki told me it's actually 17.93 miles — I might actually be more inclined to buy your story. However, it's five in the morning on a humongous day for you. Shouldn't you be sleeping or inhaling copious amounts of coffee or something?"

"Can't do that," he replies bluntly.

"Can't do what?" I'm far too sleepy for this conversation.

"It would be rude, because you can't eat or drink anything," he answers.

I roll my eyes. "It's not a big a deal. You know my eating habits are weird. You didn't have to deprive yourself just for me. None of that explains why you're here," I reply, as I go over to the round hanging chair and sit down, tucking my feet under me.

"When we talked last on the phone, you seemed nervous. I thought you might want some company until Jade and Diamond can get here."

I braid the fringe on the blanket. "My nerves are in overdrive. I've rarely gone to the doctor before this, let alone had surgery. The whole experience is strange. It's a little overwhelming."

"I'm so sorry I can't be there for you," Mark says running his hand through his short-cropped hair and pacing around my small living room. "I put Ketki in summer camp because I thought the trial might hit this week, but there was no way to plan for this too."

Something about Mark's meltdown over my cancer strikes me as funny — perhaps it's because it's five o'clock in the morning. I let out an audible snicker as I respond, "Of course you couldn't plan for this! When exactly were you supposed to plan for it … before you met me?" I ask, challenging him on his logic.

"Still, you don't have anybody. I should be there for you. It's the right thing to do."

"I'm not judging anybody — because, you know I'm not in any real position to do that — you and your friends are the *weirdest* people I've ever met … and that's saying something because I was raised in a *cult*."

He looks like he's not sure whether he wants to laugh or cross-examine me. "I think I'll ask more questions before I decide whether I'm offended."

"No, seriously! Look at it from my perspective: I've been alone for a very long time — pretty much all by myself wandering through life. One day, I stop to get a tattoo because I received spectacularly good news and instead I got pitched onto a path which completely changed my life. Okay, it's not like that's never happened to me before. I'm used to the rug being pulled out from under me."

"I'm so sorry for whatever role I've played in making this worse for you." Mark walks toward me to give me a hug.

I hold my hand to stop him. "It was a little strange, but not the strangest thing which happened that day. I walked away feeling scared and lonely, thinking to myself that normal people can call their mom and get chicken soup and have a good cry. The oncologist I saw was a jerk about the fact that I didn't have any support system around me. I couldn't explain it all to her without completely baring my soul. You've met the woman — you can understand why I didn't want to disclose anything to her. She didn't listen to me about my lack of family … just like she didn't listen when she started randomly cutting parts of me away."

The muscle in Mark's jaw visibly tightens. "Well, you don't have to deal with her anymore. You like Doctor Charleston, right? I met Hugh once when he was testifying on a colleague's case. Even though he was on the other side, his testimony was still very fair and open."

I hug one of the pillows from the chair close as I answer candidly, "Yes, he's wonderful. He took the time to carefully answer all my questions. It was great."

"Dr. Charleston is one on the best," he confirms.

"That's exactly what I'm saying. Everything with your friends has been the best. It's all been too great. Why are they this nice to me? I was simply a random customer in their shop."

Mark comes over and squats down beside the chair. "I don't know about that. I don't think there's anything random about you. Call it the teachings of my people, my personal quest in life, the things being Ketki's dad taught me — or all the above, but I don't believe in random coincidences."

"That's easy for you to say. Your coincidences haven't worked out quite like mine," I mutter under my breath

Mark shrugs. "I don't know, a fair number of them haven't been a real picnic. Anyway, as I was saying, I believe you are in my life for a reason and I am in yours for a purpose. I don't know what that purpose is. Maybe it's as simple as somebody to keep Ketki on her toes while she plays video games, or perhaps something much more profound, but we simply don't know. I can't speak for Rogue and the Ailíns', but I for one am glad you chose to come into Ink'd Deep."

"Mark, I told that quack of a doctor I didn't have a family, but you all have made a big fat liar out of me. I just think it's weird. My *own* family doesn't give a rat's ass about me — why do you guys care so much?"

"Something tells me that's part of the reason everyone cares so much. I'm almost as new around here as you are, but from what I understand family means a lot to this group. They love deeply and have lost a great deal. If they can help protect you from the evils of the world, what's the harm in letting them try?"

"Mark, what if it's worse than everyone thinks? I don't want to let everyone into my life only to hurt them later," I confess as tears gather on my lashes. I've been trying to hold back my panic and fear for days. Some days I do better than others, but the panic always starts to creep back in.

Mark notices the expression on my face and he places his warm hand over my knee and squeezes it lightly. "I truly believe you are in excellent hands. Today is the real start of your journey to kick cancer's butt. I wish I could be there, but since I can't, I brought you a little something. Hopefully, this will bring happy thoughts."

I shake my head as I chide, "Didn't we talk about this? I'm just a sometime-houseguest who your daughter absolutely annihilates at video games. You don't have to keep buying me presents."

Mark shoves his hand in his pocket in the front of his sweatshirt and removes a box. "Don't you want to see what it is first?" he teases with a boyish grin as he waves the present in front of my nose.

"Don't even try that. That's how you got me to try on those ridiculously expensive house slippers."

"You love them don't you? Come on, I promise this isn't as expensive as those, and Ketki helped me choose it."

It's like trying to fight the tide in the ocean. He's unstoppable when he sets his mind to something. Finally, I give up and stick my hand out to accept the present.

"Well, geez if you're going to pull out the big guns, a girl hardly has any choice but to say yes," I concede.

"That's exactly what I'm saying —" he agrees with a grin. "I'm glad we're on the same page now."

I carefully remove the bow and set it aside and can't even hide my squeal of approval when I peek inside the box. "It's a Teddy Bear!"

Mark looks amused. "I'm aware."

"This is going to sound incredibly stupid, but I'm twenty-eight years old and this is the first Teddy Bear I've ever had," I admit sheepishly as I carefully remove the little bear from the box. I gasp when I see the rest of the little soft sculpture. He has little-bitty patched overalls on and he's propped up against a pile of books made from felt.

"Ketki decided you would appreciate him because you are a teacher. Her favorite teacher loves to read."

"He's adorable. Thank you so much. Let me find somewhere to put this, so he doesn't break."

Mark puts his hand on my shoulder as I start to get up. "I know it looks fragile, but it's really not. I discovered this guy when I was doing some social training with Ketki when she was younger. He makes dollhouse furniture and the characters to go in them. They are incredibly durable, so feel free to take your Teddy Bear with you, if you'd like. He's the perfect pocket-sized companion."

I hand it to him. "Please put it by my purse, I don't want to forget my good luck charm." I stand up from the chair and give him a brief hug. "It means the world to me. Speaking of good luck, I hope you find the best jurors in the world and the judge sees things your way."

So cold. I'm so *frickin' cold*. It's never this way on television. After I was placed in foster care, I went on a television binging streak and watched as much TV as I possibly could. I watched everything from Tom and Jerry cartoons to unauthorized biographies and everything in between. I was particularly interested in medical horror stories because of my brother's death. As a result, I've seen a lot of footage of operations — both real and pretend — and no one ever warns you about how cold you will be.

I'm shaking so violently the scrub nurse is having a difficult time getting all the leads and monitors attached. She brings me another warm blanket and tucks it around my body. Her serious eyes constantly assess my condition. After a few moments, she checks in with me, "Feeling any warmer?"

"You can probably tell if I sugarcoat things to make this a little less awkward?" I stammer through chattering teeth.

Her eyes crinkle with mirth over her surgical mask as she confirms my hunch, "I should hope so, or I have no business in the nursing business. Tell me a bit about what's going on."

"I don't know. The blankets are helpful, but I feel like my bones are made of icicles."

"We sure don't make it easy on you, it's not a sauna in here, that's for sure. Some patients may be extra chilly because of anxiety."

"That's putting it mildly. I'm a big girl and I thought I'd be able to handle this, but I'm extremely frightened. For the first time in a long time I really wish my mom was here. That's beyond foolish, because too much water has passed under the bridge and choices have been made which can't be undone — but for today at least I wish I could turn back time."

The nurse reaches out and squeezes my hand. "I rarely run across a single soul who doesn't wish the same at one point or another, myself included. I wish I could do more, but we'll do our best to make you feel comfortable."

As much as I hate myself for it, a tear leaks from the corner of my eye. I take a deep breath and try to compose myself. "Thank you. I don't know what I would do without people like you and Dr. Charleston. Despite what it looks like, I really am okay with this. I've just never done the whole big surgery thing before. I appreciate your patience."

The nurse smiles behind her mask as she pats my arm.

"The doctor is going to give you a little medication in your I.V. now and it'll make you incredibly drowsy. I want you to think about all the happy things in your life."

Her suggestion is so similar to the one Rogue asked me a few weeks ago that it gives me pause. I'm a little stunned to realize how much my answers have changed in such a short period. Something about cancer fundamentally changes your definition of what makes you happy. It's funny, my focus seems to have changed from random things to not-so-random somebodies.

CHAPTER EIGHT

MARK

STRESS. I'M AN ATTORNEY for Pete's sake — you would think I'd be used to the concept by now. Apparently, that's not the case — my nine-year-old daughter who is usually lost in her own world just told me to take a chill pill. The irony of that is not lost on me. I am used to worrying about Ketki. I monitor everything from how much she eats, how much she sleeps, how much she exercises, to how well she does in school. It's all second nature to me. I've had to micromanage my daughter's life since Tayanita took off. It's stress, but manageable.

The situation with Shelby is a whole different ball game. I've never met somebody like her. I've been a lawyer for nearly eight years now and I've never wanted to bow out of a case as much as I do at the moment. The case isn't even progressing poorly. We're doing fairly well — this one might even be winnable. I can't be in two places at once.

The most ridiculous thing about my dilemma is that even if I could be, I don't know if Shelby would allow it. I have never seen someone be so sweetly contrary in my life. Shelby used the trial as justification to stay with Rogue and Tristan after her surgery, insisting she didn't want to interrupt my workflow and be a bother. She completely blew off any of my counterarguments. I am not exactly sure what to make of it — usually I'm a little better at this. I rarely get beaten at my own game. It's an interesting position to be in. Usually as a single attorney in a high-profile job, I am the pursued. Shelby has put me into the role of a pursuer.

At first I wasn't really sure if Ketki would be okay with a new woman. I haven't really done much visible dating around her. I didn't want to be one of those parents who has a new love interest each week. I figured Ketki might be curious about Shelby, but I didn't anticipate getting overt pressure from her to pursue a relationship. Then again, I didn't know Shelby would bond instantly with Ketki.

Sadly, many people are uncomfortable around my daughter. When Ketki is upset her movements can become erratic and loud. Although her communication style has improved since she was a small child, it's still atypical and takes a bit of getting used to.

My daughter's unusual communication style is on full display as she paces anxiously in front of me, her hands fluttering slightly before she stuffs them in her pockets.

"Dad, we *need* to get over there. Are you *ever* gonna get done with your stupid paperwork?"

I hit the save button on my laptop and close it before I respond. "What's your hurry, Ki?" I tease as she hops from one foot to the other.

"I made her peanut butter balls, because the doctor said she had to take her pain medicine with food. She usually takes her pain medicine every six hours if she got up at her usual time, it means she took her pain medicine about seven o'clock this morning. So, she probably had pain medicine with her lunch too. She needs these peanut butter cookies for her after dinner snack so she doesn't get sick."

Once again, I'm completely blown away by the things my daughter pays attention to — because sometimes it seems like she doesn't pay attention to much of anything other than her complete obsession with video games — well, those and feathers and pebbles.

"Ketki, I am so impressed that you made Shelby cookies. You know she'll love them, peanut butter is her favorite," I compliment, hoping to reinforce the social behavior.

Ketki stares at me blankly as if I've grown another head. "Duh, don't you remember the last time we made them together, she almost ate a whole pan full of cookies all by herself? Obviously, she likes them. Otherwise I wouldn't have made them for her. Come on, let's go. I want to have enough time to play games. I've heard her friend Tristan has a killer system."

"Ketki," I warn. "We're going over there to visit with Shelby. I'd prefer it if you didn't lose yourself in your games. Remember she's still tender. She's not supposed to move much. I don't know if it's safe for you guys to get involved in one of your epic video game battles. You two are like ninja warriors crossed with gymnasts when you play. Besides, you'll be a guest in Rogue's home, you can't be scoping out their video equipment. That's just rude."

Ketki rolls her eyes at me. "Dad, I know. Shelby told me all this stuff before she had the operation. I know how to be safe around her."

With every Skype call and visit with Shelby, I marvel at their relationship. Ketki is very slow to trust people and I hardly ever see her get excited over relationships with others unless they're fictional characters in her video games. It's actually quite astonishing. I set my computer down and grab the tray of cookies as we head out the door.

As I hold open the door for my daughter, I joke, "Well are you coming or do I have to wait all day?"

Ketki wrinkles her nose at me as she retorts, "Very funny Dad. I waited two hours, thirty-seven minutes and twenty-two seconds for you to be finished with your work."

I look at my watch and realize she's probably correct, but we're making progress. At least she understands I intended it to be a joke.

Ketki stops short when she sees Shelby resting on the 70's style chaise lounge in Tristan's den. She has a stack of books around her on the floor and on her lap, but it looks like she simply drifted off to sleep. I can understand why Ketki is a little taken aback. Most of Shelby's wounds are lightly covered in gauze, but the ones on her face and neck are a little more difficult to conceal, and they look angry — for lack of a better term. She's wearing a halter top with fringe so I can see the tube which was draining her deepest incisions is now gone. I try to cover my emotions because I don't want to upset Ketki, but the scene in front of me is unmistakably unsettling.

Ketki pulls on my shirt. "Is Shelby supposed to look like that? Her cuts look worse and she looks so white."

I kneel down in front of Ketki and quietly answer, "She's been through a lot and she's going to be paler than us because she's not Cherokee, remember?"

When Shelby hears our voices, she struggles to sit up. "Hey Ki, hope you brought your DS. I'm bored out of my mind."

I'm a little stunned to hear Shelby address Ketki by her pet name, but when I think about it, it's not so surprising at all. In many ways, Ketki is closer to Shelby than she is with me.

Ketki nods. "I did. But why are you so white?"

Shelby just groans. "Don't remind me about that. That's what started this whole thing or so the doctors say. When I was a teenager, my foster mom had friends with older teenage girls. I wanted to fit in and be popular. But I was one of the most backwards kids you ever saw. I knew nothing about fashion, makeup or boys. I hadn't even been to school in years. I was totally insecure. I didn't even want anybody to know about my weird past. I wanted to pretend I was somebody else. I wanted to fit into this new foster home. These people were everything my real family wasn't."

"They were?" Ketki queries.

Shelby frowns. "They were loaded with money. Sadly, their own daughter had an incurable hard to face disease they knew would kill her eventually, so for the first eight and a half years of her life, she knew she would die and they were planning for her funeral the whole time she was alive. So, when they heard the story about my brother, they figured they needed to try to adopt me."

"That was nice of them," I comment.

"One would think so, but it didn't turn out to be so

great. Instead of allowing me to be myself, they tried to turn me into the person their daughter used to be. It was a humongous mess, I didn't have any idea about who I wanted to be, and I was trying to pretend to be somebody else. I was in a household where nobody wanted me to be who I really was. It was a recipe for disaster. I became this fake teenager, trying to be older than I was. So, I did all of this weird stuff to my hair and went to tanning booths with the older girls."

"How old were you again?" I ask, trying to do the mental math in my head.

"I did about a year in temporary foster homes before I was placed with Neil and Vicki Wilcox, so I guess I was still thirteen, may be a few months shy of fourteen," I deduce.

"That's absolutely crazy. They shouldn't have allowed you to tan so young. Was Mrs. Wilcox taking you to those appointments?" I can't help it as the natural attorney-voice in me pops out.

"No, of course she wasn't. The older girls always had convenient excuses why we had to go to the mall and no one ever questioned it because teenage girls always hang out at the mall."

"Shelby, didn't the mom-lady notice you were changing color?" Ketki asks with open curiosity.

Shelby looks troubled for a moment. "You know, she probably should have, but I don't think she did. I think she was too busy with her social engagements to look closely at me. Don't get me wrong, the Wilcox family was nice. They gave me everything I needed or wanted. I thought I had everything I wanted back when I was hanging out in the middle of the wilderness with my parents, but even after I had all new stuff, I still felt empty and lonely. What I learned from the whole experience is it's not really about stuff — either no stuff, or too much stuff. You just need to find someone and a few things to make you feel cherished and comfortable. The rest of it doesn't matter."

Ketki looks baffled. "Why aren't *they* here with you? My Dad is the busiest person I've ever seen and whenever I have to go to the doctor or the hospital, he's always there."

A spark of pain crosses Shelby's face. I can tell this question is not an easy one for her to answer, yet she puts on a brave face and forges ahead, "Ketki, I don't know if I'll ever know the whole reason, but I think it's because they never got over the loss of their daughter and I couldn't compete. Sadly, I left on angry terms and we don't communicate anymore. I don't know if they would even care what I'm going through. I turned out to be simply an inconvenient blip on their radar. It's weird, I've got two sets of parents who didn't want me."

"Wow, you didn't tell me you have a mom who didn't want you too." Ketki breathes almost silently.

Shelby and I immediately protest, "Ketki, That's not exactly true — there was other stuff going on."

"Dad, if that's true for me, who's to say it's not true for Shelby too?" Ketki challenges.

Shelby swallows hard. "You're right, Ketki, I guess I don't know all the answers. I can only make guesses and they might be wrong. I've had the same cell phone number since I was twelve and no one has ever called me. I can only assume no one wants to speak to me."

"I like you and it's not just because you play video

games with me. I like talking to you and I don't like talking to most people," Ketki confesses softly.

"Oh, Ki, I love talking to you too and it's not just because you bring me cookies," Shelby responds tearfully. She leans forward in the chair to give Ketki a hug and has to draw in a deep breath as she winces in pain.

It's all I can do not to scowl at the situation and make it worse. It's the most helpless feeling in the world to see her hurting and not be able do anything about it. This isn't helping my stress level at all. There must be something I can do to help relieve her pain. In what I'm learning is very typical Shelby fashion, she merely grits her teeth and doesn't say a single word. She might not want to talk about it, but I need to see how she's really doing. It might not be the coolest thing I'll ever do in my life, but I am about to unabashedly throw Tristan under the bus as I make a suggestion to my daughter, "Hey, Ketki when I called Tristan this morning he was telling me he had new updates to his new program and he wanted players who had never seen it before to take a shot at it. Do you want to go check it out and see if you like it?"

"Dad, I thought you said we were here to hang out with Shelby, why do you want me to play video games now?" Ketki asks with an incredulous expression on her face.

"Don't worry, I'll keep Shelby company, I promise. You know me, I like to go on and on about extremely boring, complicated stuff. You might as well be having fun," I try to hedge, embarrassed at my overreaction.

"Whatever," Ketki answers as she digs a ponytail holder out of her pocket and stands in front of me waiting for me to do the usual. "You know that I know

Shelby is sick, right? She told me. It's not like she could keep it secret — the doctor dug craters all over her whole body like an archaeologist."

I nod in agreement as I finish Ketki's hair and briefly bend down to kiss the top of her head.

For the first time today, I see Shelby with her trademark wide grin. It's a little crooked because of all the swelling in her face, but she still looks beautiful. She holds her hand out to Ketki and says, "I really appreciate you looking out for me — but your dad won't do anything to hurt me. He probably wants to talk about grown-up medical stuff like what medicines I'm on or what kind of physical therapy I did last week. It's boring, tedious stuff, so you might as well go play games with Tristan. I can assure you his stuff is massively intriguing. I've been down to his little computer lab of sorts down there — it's like the set of a spy movie. Just the equipment alone is fascinating. I bet the software is downright awe-inspiring. If he gave me the chance to check it out and I felt up to it, you better believe I would be the first in line. Sadly, my skills on the computer are not as sharp as yours, so I think he'd rather have you over me."

Ketki perks up when she hears that little tidbit of information. "Really? You think so? I've been kicked out of groups on the 'net, because they don't think I know anything, because I'm just a kid or because I'm a girl."

I lay my hand on my daughter's shoulder as I respond, "I agree Ketki, it's totally not fair. So, do you want to show one of the best program designers in the whole world that you know your stuff?"

"Is pi the coolest number in the world?" Ketki asks as she sprints down the hall. That's the interesting — and sometimes perilous thing about her — she doesn't have a medium speed. It's either totally stop or totally go, nothing in between.

Over my shoulder, I comment to Shelby, "I'll be right back, I want to talk to you —"

CHAPTER NINE

SHELBY

HOW ODD. THE ALLEGEDLY hot guy on the cover of the romance novel just isn't doing it for me. Oh, I'm sure his sunny good looks, are appealing to some, but I'm finding myself drawn to an entirely different kind of man. Actually, one man. One quirky, complicated, frustrating, sometimes brooding, often amusing man. I've met no one like him. It'd be so easy to write him off as the quintessential rugged man-candy who is too good-looking for his own good, except that he's such a great dad. He's deeply spiritual in an offbeat way. In my years as a teacher's aide through college and a student teacher, I've met a lot of guys with kids, but I've never met anyone who is as close with their child as he is. It's remarkable. He juggles all of it by himself.

It would be easy for me to claim I'm not searching for a relationship. Yet if I'm honest with myself, I know that's not quite true. Deep down, I think everybody hopes they'll miraculously stumble upon the love of their life when they go to the grocery store, the post office, or out for a jog. It's supposed to happen like some grand black and white romantic movie. At least that's what I always thought when I made up stories in my head to pass the time — I'd always fantasized about growing up and meeting someone when I was grocery shopping or doing the laundry in the laundromat. My prince charming would take me away from the lifestyle I grew up in.

Of course, that was before my brother died and everything changed, but I used to dream of how someone would see me from across the room and instantly fall in love and our chemistry would be so strong nothing and no one could dissuade my potential beau from pursuing me. Back then I thought my potential foes might be dragons, wizards or monsters. I never dreamed the barriers I'd face would be both more insidious and more mundane — like chronic poverty and cancer.

Against all odds, I wonder if I have found the man of my dreams after all. Surprisingly, aside from being incredibly worried about me, Mark does not seem to believe the cancer and the fact that I might die from it is any sort of deal breaker in a relationship between us. In fact, he seems intent on flirting with me and pursuing a relationship.

It's the oddest thing about us — to the extent there is an us. One moment he seems to be openly pursuing me like any regular guy would do. The next moment, he seems to be putting on the brakes as hard as he possibly can. Yet, I'm not really in a position to be calling him out on his behavior, because I'm doing the same thing.

It would be so easy for me to settle right into a relationship, but is it really the best thing for everyone, or am I merely taking the easy road because Mark has made it so comfortable for me to stay?

It would be easier if I could simply ignore him, but Mark is everything I hoped to find in a guy. He is a man of extreme moral character; Mark isn't easily persuaded by the whims of others. If he believes something is right, he'll stand up for it regardless of what anyone else thinks. It's important for a man to have principles and be willing to stand up for them. I love the fact that he's made huge sacrifices for his daughter and is not willing to make compromises in her education or medical care. He's her biggest advocate. He's always in her corner, even when it's not convenient to be.

Mark shows the same kind of loyalty everywhere. Before he even really knew me, he extended that same dedication to me. After it became clear the first plastic surgeon I met with was subpar, Mark went out of his way to find me Dr. Charleston. It's becoming increasingly difficult for me to separate my feelings of gratitude toward Mark from something much deeper. I don't know where gratitude ends and something else begins.

What do we even call the "something else"? We are not really dating except we spend a remarkable amount of time together like a family. After the first procedure that took me by surprise, I practically moved in with Ketki and Mark. Honestly, although physically I felt like used chewing gum; emotionally, I felt the best I've been in a while. Sometimes, I get so busy living my life I forget how utterly isolated I am. Maybe, I do it intentionally, to protect myself from my own situation. I don't tell many people about the things which have happened in my life. If people ask me where my family is from, I just tell them they're not from the area. I don't often go into the long saga very much. I've revealed a shocking amount to Mark. Yet, he makes it easy to trust him with the information, because he never makes me feel like he's going to use it against me like a weapon.

Mark has gone out of his way to pamper me in a

million different ways, from making sure I have access to all of his online periodicals to getting all of my favorite foods when I was staying with him. I still can't get over the fact that he routinely cooked and cleaned for me as if it was nothing. I realize the role models I saw growing up were not the social norm, but to see the difference demonstrated in front of me, day in and day out, was nothing short of mind blowing. Ketki could sense my utter amazement and she keeps reassuring me that her dad's behavior was not unexpected — but, you could've fooled me. These characters in the romance novels have nothing on Mark Littleson, he should star in one for sure.

Just as I'm having that decadent thought, Mark enters the room. I was beginning to wonder what was taking him so long and now I'm even more concerned because his expression is thunderous. I wonder if Ketki did something to get into serious trouble. But over the last few months that I've known them, I've never seen her do anything overtly wrong. She can have an irreverent sense of humor sometimes and get a little obstinate, but I've never seen her intentionally misbehaving.

I pat the end of the chaise lounge and motion for Mark to sit down. "What's wrong? Is Ketki okay?"

For a moment, the dark expression clears from Mark's face and a slow smile emerges as he quips, "Ever heard the expression two peas in a pod? I don't think I've ever seen it applied so aptly until Tristan and Ketki met. It's like they have their own language. Ketki is positively animated. She has found her spirit guide in the human form. I'd guess Tristan is equally fascinated with Ketki."

"That sounds like a positive development. So, why do you look like you are about to toss someone in jail and throw away the key?" I ask, studying his face as it grows dark with emotion again.

Mark pulls over one of the barstools and sets it beside me before he haphazardly straddles it. "Before I answer your questions, I want to know a few answers myself," he replies, looking me over carefully.

I squirm under his perusal before I finally reply, "What? Stop giving me the once over. I'm basically fine for somebody who had major surgery. This isn't anything they didn't tell me about ahead of time."

"Okay, fair enough," he answers with the tight nod of his head. "Now, instead of telling me what you think I want to hear, tell me how you really feel."

"How I feel is *frustrated*. I want to throw my hands up in the air, but I can't because it hurts to move my arms. I want to take a nice long hot shower, but I can't do that either, because I'm supposed to be taking sponge baths until my incisions heal completely. I'm not even allowed to walk around or do my yoga because I might tear my incisions open and they would have to re-do them."

I have to stop as a violent shudder rolls through my body. Mark whispers in a low growl, "Oh God Shel." I don't even know if he's aware he uttered a sound as he scoots even closer to support me.

That little innocuous act gives me strength to continue my story. "Do you know I had to use a wheelchair when I went in to have the little drains removed from my incisions because they didn't want me to bear much weight on my legs? I'm ashamed of myself. You know, I thought I wasn't a vain person — but what does all this say about me? I have this freakin' cancer because I was pursuing an ideal sort of skin color which may or may not even exist in nature. I wasn't happy with who I was so I pretended to be somebody else. Because I did, I have cancer. How stupid is that? So you would think I would learn my lesson."

"You need to —" Mark starts to interrupt.

I plow right through his words and continue speaking. I need to get my story out and tell him about how I feel before I can't. "But now …now I can't even stand to look at my body in the mirror. The health nurse is supposed to come by and check things out. I can't even bring myself to show her my skin — I'm afraid of what she'll say. I don't feel strong enough to take a closer look on my own. She may pack up the hospital bed Tristan so generously rented for me and make me go back to the hospital. When I told her my symptoms, she wasn't pleased with how a few of my incisions seem to be healing. I swear, I've been very compliant with Dr Charleston's instructions. I've tried the best I can. I am so scared."

Mark gently gathers my hand in his own and kisses the back of my knuckles as he declares, "*Immokalee*, I am so sorry. If I could take the fear from you, I would."

His simple straightforward declaration makes me smile through my tears. "You know, I'm not prone to believe the promises of other people. I'm pretty self-reliant, but I honestly believe you would if it was in your power. You've done so much for me, it's incredible. I am so grateful you and Ketki are in my life."

"We are at that, aren't we — but I guess the question is what role do you want us to play in your life?"

For a moment I'm completely stunned into silence. Although, for the life of me I can't understand why. I should've expected this from Mark. He is the kind of person who tackles every problem head-on. If he doesn't understand something he will ask you a million questions until he knows the answer — Ketki definitely gets that skill from him. I guess it shouldn't surprise me he would transfer his skills over to his personal life as well. It certainly isn't one of those fluffy, light romantic scenes from the romance books Jade and Rogue bought me to pass the time since my surgery. Nothing at all flowery and ethereal about this. This is purely a fact-finding mission. Facts. If I examine the facts, there is only one conclusion I can draw. Mark looks almost stoic as he waits for me to process his question — stoic — but with a tinge of worry, if that is possible.

Smiling at him, I gently squeeze his hand as I announce, "Well, that's the easiest question I'm likely to answer all day. If you're willing to have me with all of my problems and drama in your life, I'd like to be part of yours."

Mark seems a little shell-shocked by my answer. I can't say I blame him. I have been a little erratic in my approach. That's a bit of an understatement. I have given him more faulty starts than a yo-yo on an elementary school playground.

He drops my hand for a moment and leans back. "I'll probably kick myself for this in a minute. Unfortunately, it's part of who I am. I need to make sure you understand where I'm coming from here, okay? It's not because of who you are — I hope you understand —"

"Mark — remember, I'm a math major. Do you think I'd criticize you for analyzing a situation?" I interrupt, with more than a hint of amusement. "Although, your timing sucks."

Finally, he seems to relax a little and smile. "Right. I

knew there was a reason we get along so well. I want to make sure you know Ketki and I are a package deal. I figure you do, but I thought I had the same understanding with someone once before and it didn't turn out that way, so I just want to make sure I'm clear."

Mark usually does a good job of masking his emotions. I'm sure it's a skill he has learned over time as an attorney. I don't suppose you can let the jury see every thought which crosses your mind. Still, I can see the open anxiety on his face. It must be hard to have to live your life so shielded from everyone. I know he tries hard to protect Ketki from emotional extremes because it impacts her behavior. But he seems to feel like he has to keep things under wraps everywhere.

I would love to hop up and give him a huge hug to let him know how much I want to be in his life and in his arms. You know what? The heck with it — I'm not going to let a little melanoma take this moment away from me. I have to stop and untangle myself from all the pillows and ice packs I'd been using to prop myself up and ice myself down to help control swelling.

Mark is watching my gyrations with concern. When he sees me trying to launch myself from the somewhat awkward chaise lounge, he dives toward me to offer me his hand to support me. "Shelby … what are you doing?" he asks with alarm, as he keeps me upright.

I'm not sure if it's the emotional intensity of the situation, my pain medication or the lingering effects of the surgery, but I'm feeling quite unstable. He seems to sense this and pulls me closer and tucks me under his chin. After I take a couple of steadying breaths, I step back.

"I want to answer you properly. It may not have

occurred to you, but we are having a 'moment' here and I need to make my intentions clear."

Mark's eyebrows raise to an impressive height, but he says nothing.

"I know we're still getting to know each other, but there are a few things which are crystal clear about you. You are a man of precise intention and integrity. You don't leave very many things open for misinterpretation. Through every word, action and interaction, you've made it clear you care very much about my well-being. I can't ask for much more in a partner. Even so, I get so much more with you. I get to see you interact beautifully with your daughter and nurture her into a beautiful thriving human being. It's not often someone gets to see love in motion, but that's what I get to see between you and Ketki."

Mark swallows hard and draws in a deep breath.

"That's the second thing I know without a doubt. You guys are like peanut butter and jam. I would never dream of asking one of you to be present in my life without the other. It would just be wrong. The two of you belong together. I know you're a package deal. I wouldn't have it any other way. Anyone who thinks it could be otherwise, has never watched the two of you together."

Mark clears his throat roughly and shuffles his feet. His voice breaks with emotion. "Shelby, I hate to —"

I place my finger over his lips before I interject, "Stop! I can almost guess what you're going to ask me. So you can just stop. I might be a special education teacher, but if you remember correctly, when I first met you, I didn't even know about Ketki yet."

"Yeah? So?" he asks cautiously. "What does that mean for us?"

"In case you didn't notice, I was wildly attracted to you before I knew you were a hot dad. I liked you just fine on your own, without Ketki."

"No, I didn't notice. I was too busy making a fool out of myself."

I stand on my tiptoes and brush a kiss across Mark's lips. "I think the two of us have been playing that game."

I feel like I'm going to throw up. I can't believe I'm back in the same spot of uncertainty again. I thought that's why I've gone through this twice already. "Did they give you any more information about why they wanted to see me?" I probe as I push the delicate pieces of crêpe around my plate. I'm sure if I actually had an appetite, this would be delicious. Unfortunately, food tastes disgusting right now and the very idea of it seems repulsive.

Mark silently observes my behavior for a few moments before he offers me his plate of buttermilk pancakes. "Want to trade?"

His calm demeanor is driving me crazy. How can he sit there eating breakfast when our whole lives may be blowing up in our faces? I take a deep breath as I respond, trying desperately to stay sweet, although I feel anything but. "No, no thanks. I'm not hungry this morning."

"You need to eat." Mark chastises. "The doctor said it was important for you to keep your weight up to be able to fight off everything."

"Look, I said I wasn't hungry, okay?" I snap. "I've

got way too much to think about to worry about whether I'm packing on calories."

Mark sighs, but says nothing.

"I don't understand what they could need to talk about. I thought we had all the best people there helping us. The person was beyond vague on the phone. It was some mumbo-jumbo about proper protocol being breached and records being compromised, but not to be overly concerned because it was something they've dealt with many times before. What kind of Psychobabble is that? It all seems crazy to me. What if my parents had it right all along?" I ask, my voice breaking with emotion.

Mark slides around the circular vinyl booth until he's sitting right next to me. He puts his arm around me and tucks me in next to his shoulder before he asks, "Shelby, what's going on? You've had scary visits to Dr. Charleston before and you never seemed quite this unnerved."

"I don't know. It felt like they were lying to me about something." I reply, shivering at the memory. "I guess this is feeling a lot like my childhood."

"What do you mean?" Mark asks as he pours me a little tea and doctors it with honey.

"Growing up, it seems like my whole life was one big pursuit around how to make my brother better — at least that's how it started out before my parents discovered Reverend Frachett. At first, we were a relatively normal family. We started traveling from revival service to revival service and church to church, so pastors could pray for him to make him better. Most of the legitimate pastors could see there was something seriously wrong with Owen and urged my parents to take him to the hospital."

I fiddle with the teacup.

Mark reaches out to gently still my hands.

"I was too little to understand why my dad wasn't able to maintain a job and so they didn't have health insurance and they were too paranoid to believe in signing up for government assistance, even basic needs. Over time, the more reputable pastors began to fall away. We began to travel farther and farther away to seek out people on the fringe who would tell my parents exactly what they wanted to hear. Some stuff was outrageous. Even as a child I could tell it was certainly not true — but other things I never actually knew whether the claims were true or false."

"It must've been terribly confusing for you."

"Oh, you've no idea! Savannah and I were just kids, but we started feeling like it was our responsibility to protect our parents from themselves. It was not only confusing, it was scary. I remember as soon as I learned what money was, I started hiding it away because my parents felt like 'God' was telling them to give these people all of our money we'd managed to scrape together for food."

Mark grits his teeth and shakes his head as he stirs his coffee.

"I understand the Bible says not to be boastful about money, but being able to pay for milk, eggs and a few Cheerios is not the same as lusting after money. For some reason my parents didn't understand. In every new town we went to in search of a miracle cure for my brother, they were subjected to a new round of fleecing. It was absolutely insane."

"Why didn't anyone else from your town say

anything?" Mark is alert with curiosity. "Wasn't it obvious your brother wasn't doing very well?"

I feel the blood drain out of my face as dozens of moments flood my memory like a deranged kaleidoscope. I can't help but let out a dry laugh as I respond, "Obvious? Oh yeah. Sad? It didn't get much sadder. Sometimes horrific. I remember him looking so frail that it looked as if you could see through his skin. At one point, I used to pray to myself for a well-meaning adult to stop and ask questions. I would get my hopes up if someone would stop and ask for the time. Sadly, there weren't any heroes in our story. It was as if no one could actually see us. We needed a village of heroes, but what we got was a world of disinterested bystanders."

"Shelby, I'm sorry. I didn't mean to bring all that up." Mark tucks his jacket around my shoulders when he sees me shiver.

"Mark, it's not just you. It's this whole situation. It's going from one specialist to another and having them promise things which are turning out not to be true. It makes me feel like I did when we were young going from one church to the next. It feels the same and I'm beginning to wonder if anybody knows what they're talking about. What if this melanoma isn't even curable? What if I've let it go on too long?"

"Shelby, there are so many factors with cancer. It's hard for anybody to give you an answer with any degree of certainty. It depends on your environment, your genetics and plain old luck. Do you even know anything about your family's history with cancer?"

I throw up my hands in frustration and am again reminded what's already happened as one of my deeper incisions on my back pulls uncomfortably and sends a long twinge of pain through my side and under my arm.

"I don't really know anything about my family. The things I used to know about them were seen through the eyes of a twelve-year-old. It probably wasn't correct information even then," I sadly shake my head. "For all I know, my whole family could be dead. I could be the last person to get cancer instead of the first person."

"That's a lot of guessing to do based on a single phone call. Maybe the news isn't quite as bad as you're anticipating. All we can do is deal with what comes," Mark tries to reassure me.

"Logically, I know you're probably right, but I'm beyond logic. Right now, I'm scared spitless. I'm sorry to break it to you, but you're just going to have to deal with me being a basket case. You know what sucks about this? Ketki comes home from camp today and I was looking forward to spending time with her. Now I'll be in a weird headspace and she'll totally pick up on it."

Mark sighs deeply. "We've got bigger problems. I just got a message from Susan. She's heard from her sources in the courtroom that the judge is about to order a change of venue in my trial. At this point, we're not sure where, but it could very likely be in Ocala, which would be about an hour away."

"Wow, that's gonna throw a wrinkle in things," I remark softly.

Mark looks at me with a raised eyebrow. "You think? The daughter of mine is not big on change to her routine. I'm not sure how to handle this. Since it's summer break, I could take her with me. She'd have to stay at the hotel while I was in trial. If the judge has taken the extraordinary step to move the trial after we've already started selecting the jury, it's likely he'll sequester everyone, even though Ocala is only less than an hour away from Gainesville. Ketki would probably be okay with that as long as she had Internet access. As a dad, I don't think I'm okay with it. I guess I could ask my sister to watch her."

A giggle escapes me as I see the sour expression on his face. "Something tells me that's not your favorite option either —"

Mark scrapes his hand down his face as he answers, "Let me put it this way. I love my sister very much, but my daughter and I don't love soap operas nearly as much as Leoti does. Whenever she watches Ketki, I always have to hear about the huge sacrifice Ketki made to stay with her. I used to brush off Ketki's complaints, but about three years ago, I got the stomach flu and I had to stay with my sister for a couple days. Let's just say I am a lot more sympathetic about Ketki's complaints after my experience."

"I completely understand. My foster mom was a complete soap opera addict. She even watched a television channel dedicated to nothing but soap operas. She had all the characters from four or five of them completely memorized and seemed to think they were real. I had never watched television before so it was a novel and somewhat scary experience for me." A random thought strikes as I see the stress lines on his face. "Do you need to go and deal with this? I can go to this appointment by myself. I've been on my own for a long time. You didn't need to take the whole morning off just to be with me."

"Immokalee, I needed to. It's been a while since I've been in a relationship, but I'm pretty sure this is how it's

done. I would feel like a colossal jerk if I was just sitting around in my office waiting for a ruling from the judge which may or may not even come down today while you were getting critical news about your future. I've got law clerks, associates and partners to help me. I've only got one you, and I choose to be here with you. Is that a problem?"

Something about his awkward statement touches my heart and I tear up. "No, I don't have a problem with it. I'm not used to being anyone's first priority."

"Well, get used to it because that's the way you deserve to be treated, Shelby."

"I hope you feel the same when I offer to watch Ketki for you while you're in trial —" I counter.

"Are you sure you're up to it? My daughter can be a handful," Mark warns.

"I'm all about the package deal, remember?" I reply with a watery smile. "Besides, I happen to think your daughter is all kinds of cool all on her own. She's good for my outlook on life."

CHAPTER TEN

MARK

"Littleson, you found yourself A gem of a woman at my tattoo shop," Marcus comments as he tightens the screws on the bunk-bed we're putting together at Shelby's little cottage. "Maybe I should start a dating service."

I throw my head back and laugh. "Didn't you get yourself in a little bind with a dating service? I'm surprised Rogue still talks to you at all after what you pulled. I know if you did that to my sister, she would put you on her do-not-call list *forever.*"

Isaac chuckles as he joins the conversation, "It was the recipe for a major disaster, but everyone ended up happy in the end and I found my family again, I can't be upset about this one's harebrained scheme. Much to my surprise, he's been a fine son-in-law. He loves my daughter, Ivy."

I turn to Tristan who is busy building a student desk for Ketki. "I understand you track down people."

Tristan nods. "Yes, that's part of what Identity Bank does."

"Could you track down a family who completely rejects technology?" I ask carefully forming the question around the thoughts which have been tumbling around in my brain for weeks.

"You looked troubled, son." Isaac studies me. "Is your case giving you problems?"

"No, this isn't about work at all. This is a much more personal mission. That's why I'm not sure how to proceed. Usually, at work, I can follow a prescribed way of doing things and the outcome is predictable. Unfortunately, I don't think that's the case here. I'm not even sure if this is the right path to take. I'm trying to help Shelby, but this step may not be helpful at all. I simply don't know."

"What do you mean?" Marcus asks, "I thought Ivy told me Shelby has no family. I guess I'm just lost in this situation as usual."

"Lost is a good word for it I suppose," I explain. "Shelby's early life was a bit reminiscent of a Charles Dickens novel and she was removed from her family by the authorities. No one has tried to locate her, but she doesn't know if the move was purposeful or accidental. What I don't know how to ascertain is whether helping her find them again would be beneficial to her recovery."

"Wow, that's a big move," Marcus observes.

"I haven't talked much about my background, but I'm Cherokee. My people have a belief in something called *tohi*. In fact we use the same word for health and balance in our language. Rather than try to merely 'fix' Shelby's symptoms, like in Western medicine, my people would encourage her to find healing and balance in the rest of her life. I can't help but wonder if reuniting her with her family might help her feel more whole and complete. Perhaps it would be one more tool to help her battle her cancer. I'm not suggesting it would be a replacement for everything else, family is just another piece of the puzzle. She needs more people on her side in this battle. She needs *tohi*."

Tristan's eyebrows come together and his face sets in grim determination as he thinks for a few moments before giving an answer, "What does Shelby think about this? I have to tell you, Mark, I've seen adoption reunions like this go very well or blow up like a military ordinance. It's a scary thing planning these because you might think you have one kind of situation and it turns out to be the other way around."

I heave a deep breath as Tristan vocalizes my every fear. "Exactly! That's why I haven't done anything so far — but what if reuniting with them helps give her strength to fight? What if they can provide answers for the doctors?"

"Do you have any idea what we might find if we look?" Isaac asks.

"I only have the barest of outlines. When she was twelve, she had a mom, a dad and an older sister Savannah. Her youngest brother, Owen, passed away under odd circumstances."

Tristan runs his hand through his hair. "I suppose it would be enough for me to do a preliminary inquiry to see what's out there. I wouldn't need to make huge waves. I can just do enough to check what kind of situation Shelby might be facing."

I breathe a sigh of relief. "That sounds like a decent plan. If it's devastating information, we don't have to ambush her with it and if it's potentially helpful, then we've laid some groundwork for a reunion. I'd like to see if I can help bring her a bit of inner peace. Thank you for your help."

"You know, you're going to have to tell your girlfriend what's going on. Sooner or later, she'll find out. It's probably better you tell her in advance," Marcus advises. "Being married has taught me secrets aren't ever a good thing."

"I've learned the hard way too," I comment. "I'm just trying to protect Shelby from any more pain."

"I know your intentions are good," Isaac replies sympathetically, "Sadly, that's not always possible."

"Dad, I thought you had a huge trial this summer? What happened?" Ketki asks as she separates her French fries by size, laying them out on a napkin.

"Trial stuff can sometimes be complicated," I try to explain. "It turns out the judge decided there was too much local news coverage about the people in this case and the jury members could not be fair, so he moved the trial somewhere else. That's not an easy thing to do. It messed up some people's schedules because the judge decided the people involved need to stay in a hotel and be completely away from media attention. So, they had to postpone the trial for a bit."

"That's good, right?" Ketki asks.

I chuckle softly before I answer, "I don't know. There are a bunch of law review articles and case studies about whether the change of venue helps or hurts my side."

"No silly, I'm not talking about your case. I'm talking about Shelby. Now you'll be around when she has to go in and have another operation. She can stay with us again instead of having to stay at Rogue's house."

"I suppose you're right. If Shelby wants to, she could stay with us — but it must be her choice," I answer carefully, not wanting to get Ketki's hopes up.

Ketki's silent for a couple of minutes before she adds, "Maybe Shelby is just scared of us."

"What do you mean, Ki?" I ask, curious about her theory.

"Well, you know how some teachers are super nice and a few teachers are not so nice? During the summer, you never know which kind of teacher you'll get when school comes — so you worry and worry all summer until school starts. Every teacher always says it'll be a great school year, but it doesn't always turn out that way. Maybe she feels the same way about us. She told me she hasn't had very many boyfriends … maybe she's scared."

It takes me a moment to form words as I study my daughter. Beneath her crooked braids — I guess I should've taken a little while longer this morning to put them in — and her all-too-brief smiles, you would never guess there is a wise little philosopher buried deep in there. "Ketki, I think you might actually be on to something. The question is, what do we do about it?"

Ketki shrugs as she responds, "I guess you do the same thing with Shelby as you do with me when something scares me. You show it to me over and over again in different settings to prove it's okay and it won't hurt me. We just have to prove to her we're not the bad guys. That should be easy enough, right? I play a lot of role-playing games and I know we're not the bad guys."

I grin at my daughter. "You're absolutely right. If I can't convince my girlfriend I am a good guy, I am in serious trouble."

Shelby is looking less than amused as she climbs into my car. This is not an auspicious start to "Operation Good Guy."

"Good evening, Shelby. You look gorgeous as usual," I say in greeting as I walk around the car to help her in.

Shelby openly scoffs. "Mark, you might want to get your vision checked. In case you haven't noticed, Diamond and I have been working in the stacks all day today. I am an absolute wreck. I have never seen so much dust in my life. All I want is a shower and a bed."

I quickly consult my watch and mentally kick myself. I probably should have timed this a little better but I am discovering that juggling a dating life with a preteen and a career is a little more challenging than I had anticipated. "Can I offer you a compromise?" I offer. "How about a quick shower and a surprise?"

Shelby sighs deeply before she reluctantly responds, "Is there food involved in this surprise? I am starving. Lunch was abysmal."

Sliding my courtroom demeanor on, I calmly answer, "Of course there is, I wouldn't let you starve."

Boy, you have the moves down Littleton, how long has it been since you dated? I think to myself as I quickly evaluate my options to cover up my colossal oversight. Why can I manage a complex trial but not be able to get a handle on my own personal life?

Shelby rolls her shoulders and neck as she answers, "All I can say is that this surprise better be good, because today has been a rough one."

"I'm hoping this surprise will ease some of your pain." I reach out and rub a knot from the back of her neck.

Shelby leans into my hand. "Nice. I could do with a little less pain in my life."

"After the way I grew up, I never thought I'd believe a picnic on the beach would be a fun thing again. This is amazing. How in the world did you pull all of this off? I'm amazed Ketki didn't spill the beans. Your daughter is like a walking, talking tabloid."

I grin tightly. "It took a little doing. There might have been a promise of new video games involved," I add sheepishly.

Shelby snorts with laughter. "Well, whatever it takes, this is lovely and the food is delicious."

I nod as I take a bite. "Yeah, Frannie's is a perennial favorite at Ink'd Deep. I owe Declan big time for the recommendation."

I owe him more than that, but Shelby doesn't need to know all the details. While she was showering, I was busy trying to cover my dating gaffe. I haven't been this clumsy at the dating game since I was about thirteen. I can't believe I've forgotten the tenets of Basic Dating 101, like *Feed Your Date*.

In my defense, when arranging all of this, I spent a great deal of time dealing with one of Ketki's meltdowns. Even though Ketki is brilliant when it comes to mathematics and problem-solving, sometimes when it comes to personal relationships, things are more difficult to explain. My daughter was devastated because I wanted to hang out with Shelby without her. It was a difficult departure this evening for sure. Even preparing Ketki in advance didn't seem to lessen the conflict. I hope this is a momentary blip and not an indication how things will go if things get serious between Shelby and I. It would be an impossible dilemma.

An excited shriek breaks through my inner musings. "You didn't tell me we were going to see Jade's fiancé! I am so excited. They talk about Declan all the time. That's funny, Diamond didn't say anything either. Jett just came by on his motorcycle and told her she needed to 'get in gear or she would be late,' I suppose everybody's here. This will be spectacular!"

I don't blush often. Even so I feel my face heating as I pull her back against my chest and murmur in her ear, "Anything to make you happy, I aim to please. I'm a good guy that way —"

"I'm not sure why my friends say good guys are boring, It's simply not true at all …"

CHAPTER ELEVEN

SHELBY

As strange as it may seem, some days I wonder if getting cancer might have been a blessing in disguise as they say. I can't even believe I'm having that thought. Yet, I know deep down it's true. Had I not let my guard down in front of Mark on the terrible, awful day I received my news, none of the rest of this would've ever happened. *This.* This is what I dreamed of when I would sneak away by myself and write stories about how I hoped my life would turn out.

I snuggle down into the thick comforter and roll toward Mark. I still can't believe he arranged such an elaborate surprise. The concert was like something you might see on some music channel on TV. Jade's fiancé, Declan, called us up on stage to slow dance to one of his ballads he wrote for Jade. It was the most romantic thing I had ever seen — all of Jade's friends were there and we danced to her song. After all Jade and her friends have done for me, it was such an honor to be included in such a personal moment. I'm amazed how naturally Mark and I fit into the group. It's almost as if we've been friends for decades.

After the concert, Mark asked me how I wanted to

handle the rest of the evening. In some ways, this was an odd question because Mark has already seen me at my most raw and exposed. Yet last night was unlike anything we had quite encountered before. It was a "close my eyes and jump kind of moment." It might not be the smartest thing I've ever done, but to be honest, I didn't spend a lot of time weighing the alternate consequences of my actions. It was a pretty simple equation in my mind. Mark was a really good guy on a mission to take great care of me, for once I was going to let him do that, however he wanted to.

My body heats and flushes a little as I remember how well he took care of me last night. I snuggle closer to his chest and let out a soft sigh.

"What are you thinking about, *Immokalee*?" he asks with a tender grin.

"Oh nothing," I respond, burying my head in the pile of blankets next to his chest.

I feel his chest rumble with laughter as he teases, "Come on, are you going to lie to an officer of the court?" He pulls me up to a sitting position next to him as he continues sounding more serious, "I bet you're thinking about the same thing I'm thinking about — which is how absolutely perfect we are together. I know you'll probably think this is a cheesy morning-after line, but please believe me when I say I have never had this kind of connection with anybody, ever."

Before I can censor what I'm about to say, I hear myself ask, "What about Ketki's mom?" I want to disappear. I don't know what made me ask such a stupid question; I'm not that kind of woman. Yet, the question is just hanging there in the air like a pair of stinky socks. *Way to kill the mood Shelby...*

Mark is silent for so long I'm certain I've done serious damage to the sweet romantic mood — at the very least. Just as I'm about to open my mouth to issue the most epic of all apologies, he starts to speak, "I suppose if I was in your shoes, I'd want to know too. It's a fair question. I guess the short answer is Tayanita and I were different people back then — both young and ambitious. We were good friends when we got married, to be sure. Yet, in retrospect, maybe we were both a little too anxious to get married and get on with the business of life before we knew what the business of life was like."

"I'm sorry Mark, it's not really any of my concern — " I start to apologize.

Mark shrugs as he continues with his story, "It's okay, it seems like it was a lifetime ago. We were so young. We hadn't even talked about what our expectations of marriage were. Our families had been friends for generations and everyone always assumed we would get married. Since we liked each other, we saw no reason not to. We thought we could build a solid life together. I didn't realize we were not only on totally different pages, we were reading from completely different books. If I had known she never wanted any children, I probably wouldn't have agreed to marry her."

His explanation of his relationship with his ex-wife is different from what I expected. I guess I thought he might absolutely hate her for rejecting Ketki. "Are you always this levelheaded about it all? I'm impressed because I guess I'd be much more ticked off."

"Honestly, I don't think about her too much anymore. For a long time, I wondered if she would change her mind and show up at my front door with her moving boxes. It seems like the timeframe for that has passed by now, don't you think?" he asks philosophically. "If she had a sense of undying love for me and her daughter, she would've been around by now. I guess it's her loss. I suppose if I had to deal with her every day and have her in my face to remind me of what happened, it might be a different story, but she's just gone. We can't miss what isn't here," Mark explains.

"Well, I give you massive kudos for being a very grown up grown-up. I'm not sure I would be so generous. I'll try not to give her a piece of my mind if we ever have the misfortune of being face-to-face. I think what she did to you and Ketki is despicable. Ketki is amazing and she did not deserve to be discarded like yesterday's trash," I sputter indignantly.

Mark draws big circles on my back with his hands being careful to avoid any of my sore spots. He took such a careful catalog of all of my pain last night. It was like he worshiped every inch of me. He kisses the top of my head. "*Immokalee*, do we really want to waste the time we have together talking about my ex-wife? I can think of much more productive ways to use it."

As usual, Mark makes an excellent point. I ignore the twinges in my ribs and back as I throw the blankets off his chest and throw my leg over his so I'm straddling him. As I kiss his jaw and chest, I look up coyly. "You're right. This is a much more productive use of my time."

The air is stale and it tastes like chemicals. Someone has tried to make the environment less clinical by hanging a few pieces of brightly colored abstract art on the wall. Unfortunately, it doesn't evoke the feeling of home, it just feels out of place and wrong. Everything about this place is a reminder of the pain and suffering I'll experience one more time. It completely blows my mind that I have to start again from scratch. I worked so hard on my rehab. I can't believe I went through all that for nothing. I hate thinking in circles. I've been doing it for days. One minute I'm fine and the next minute, I'm so angry I can't think. I'm angry because my body betrayed me. I'm angry because one little PET scan has the power to change my whole life. I'm even more angry at the life choices I made to bring me to this point.

I try to distract myself from my disappointment by talking to Mark about inane stuff. "I couldn't believe it the other day when Jade told me the story of her engagement. It's amazing that she had the presence of mind to say yes. I would get so nervous I wouldn't even remember my own name."

Mark squeezes my hand. It feels weird because at the same time, the blood pressure cuff is automatically taking my blood pressure. I hate all these crazy machines. How do I even know they're doing their jobs correctly? Yet, no one else seems remotely concerned or alarmed, so I focus on taking a deep breath and breathing through it all.

"Shelby, Dr. Charleston was totally baffled by the fact that the PET scan had not been done before this surgery. He is not sure whose results he was shown, but they weren't yours. Dr. Charleston is not happy with the hospital and basically read them the riot act. He threatened to pull his credentials from this hospital if they don't tighten their protocols."

"That doesn't help me much, does it? I still have to have surgery yet another time," I snap, feeling panic over take me.

"I'm sorry I can't make that part go away for you too,

I wish I could. I've got a team at Hunters Crossing looking into ways to make the hospital sit up and take notice of their protocol," Mark growls under his breath.

"Is that a fancy way of telling me you're planning to sue the pants off of them?" I whisper, my eyes wide with shock. "I didn't think you guys did that kind of thing at your office."

"We've been looking into expanding our clientele," he answers succinctly.

Mark and I both jump about a foot in the air when we are interrupted by a nurse. "Excuse me, Ms. Lyons, I just want to let you know Dr. Holtz, the anesthesiologist, has been delayed a few minutes."

Her voice is instantly recognizable. I look up to see a set of familiar brown eyes. I eagerly tap Mark on the shoulder as I announce, "Mark, remember I told you about that cool nurse who helped me keep calm when I was losing my mind on the operating table the last time I was in here? This is her! I can't believe it."

I turn to the scrub nurse and earnestly declare, "I'm so glad I ran into you again. I never got a chance to say thank you for helping me keep it together that day. I was so scared. You helped me so much! I'm sorry, I never got your name because I was so groggy."

Mark lets out a deep heaving sigh as he sits forward in his chair, shaking his head. He and the nurse both look like they've been hit in the solar plexus.

"Shelby," he says, after pausing a few moments to regain his speech, "Remember when I told you there must be forces bigger than us involved with our meeting? Meet the next exhibit —"

"Mark, what are you talking about?" I ask,

completely befuddled.

"I mean — my brother, karma or the spirits must be having some fun now because your favorite nurse happens to be my ex-wife, Tayanita."

"Wow. Just wow. Did you *know* she was a nurse?" I stammer after a few moments. "Did you arrange for her to work on my case? I'm sorry I'm just terribly confused."

"No, there's no way he could have," the woman supplies in a rather shaky voice. "The last time I spoke to Mark, I was still getting my ears wet as a CNA. He would've had no idea that I've worked my way up to the rank of surgical nurse."

"So, you guys don't talk at all? Like not at all — you don't even know how Ketki is doing?"

Tayanita slumps against the door frame as she answers, "No, I don't know. I figure I forfeited the right to find out about my daughter when I was foolish enough to walk out the door. I just couldn't find a way to balance who I was with what my daughter needed from me and I lost myself and my daughter in the process. It took me a while to figure it all out and when I did, I figured it would be better for everyone if I simply stayed away."

As I watch the emotions play across the face of the woman I thought I would never understand, something utterly shocking happens. I begin to feel sorry for my former sworn enemy. She seems truly regretful. She's not at all the monster I envisioned her to be. "That must've been tough," I sympathize.

Tears spring to her eyes. "I'm sorry. I can't do this at work. If you want me to be transferred off your case, I guess it could be arranged."

I hold up my hand to get her attention. "Tayanita,

please stop. The only reason I brought you to Mark's attention to begin with is because I thought you did an exceptional job as a nurse. It would be silly for me to ask for someone new because you guys know each other. I know you're a professional. I will see you in a few minutes. Hopefully, you won't have to talk me down from the ceiling this time. Although if you have to, I have no doubt you can."

Tayanita nods her head toward me in acknowledgment. "All right then Ms. Lyons. I'll see you back in the operating theater. Hopefully, this time won't be as traumatizing for you since you know what to expect. Thank you for your kindness."

She turns toward Mark. "This one is nice. She'll probably treat you better than I did."

CHAPTER TWELVE

MARK

IF YOU HAD TOLD me my two worlds would collide like this, I would've laughed in your face. I never thought it would happen in a million years. How ironic is it that the woman I loved in my past is taking care of the person I can see loving in the future? I can't even begin to wrap my brain around all the coincidences which needed to unfold in the universe for it to occur.

I didn't even know my ex-wife was seriously considering nursing as a career. Last I knew, she was doing CNA work because it was a way to make some quick money. She hated working retail, and one of my classmates in law school mentioned they made a big shift differential by working CNA jobs at nights and on the weekends. It worked well for us to work opposite shifts after Ketki was born. Tayanita was more than willing to work nights for the extra money — I'm shocked she elected to make a career out of it.

According to Shelby, she's a great nurse. Yet, I still struggle with the idea that she can care so much for one group of people and so little for her own daughter. I don't know how to make sense of the disparity. I don't know what I thought she was doing with her life, but caring for people wasn't it. I guess I figured she was a high-powered executive moving stocks on the stock exchange or something equally impersonal. The fact that she cares for people for money but is unable to care for our own daughter sticks in my craw in a way I can't explain. Why can't she do both? Why after all these years didn't she reach out and say, "Hey, I've made peace with myself and my decisions?"

I'm pacing back-and-forth in front of the fountain of a nondescript park. I feel like I'm waiting for an illicit drug deal to go down instead of a conversation I should've had with my ex-wife years ago. I hate that I lied to virtually everyone to make this conversation happen. I certainly wasn't going to tell my sister about Tayanita when I dropped Ketki off. The resulting can of worms would've been so large, I would've never been able to get the lid on. Instead, I made a vague comment about running errands.

Rogue and Jade are entertaining Shelby at the house today. Her recovery from this operation has been rough. It's so much harder on her than the last one — and the last one was downright hellish. Her friends are trying their best to distract her from the pain and boredom of having to stay completely immobile. Her incisions this time are deeper and more extensive, so she must stay inactive. This is not Shelby's style. It's driving her absolutely crazy.

Finally, I come to rest on an old wrought-iron bench and try to concentrate on checking phone messages from work. I'm about to throw in the towel and declare my efforts completely ineffective when Tayanita comes up beside me and brushes an air kiss near my cheek. "I would say that happy looks good on you Mark, but right now you look ready to murder your phone."

"I am. I hate trying to read this thing in the sunlight," I admit. "Enough of the small talk. Fancy meeting you here or anywhere —" I begin with more than a trace of bitterness in my voice.

For a moment, Tayanita looks as if I've slapped her but then she straightens her spine and answers. "I know. It's definitely one of those stranger than fiction moments. I'm sorry about Shelby though. She seems like a phenomenal person."

"She is. She's one of the best. I'm really frustrated. I can't get anyone to give me a concrete answer about her cancer. Why won't anybody simply spell it out in black and white for me?"

"Mark, I'm sorry we can't. The best we can do is give you vague statistics about the number of people who beat the disease but we can't tell you who or why. Anything else would be a lie. I wish we could make promises but every case is individual. There are no black-and-white answers with cancer. We're getting closer with things like gene therapy — it's better than it used to be, but we're not there yet. I can tell how much Shelby means to you, and if I could give you answers, I would. Unfortunately, I can't."

"It's so ironic. For *years* I waited for you to come back into my life. My life was completely vacant, there was room for you to find yourself and come back — but you didn't. For almost seven years — you didn't come back. I don't even know what to think. How in the world could you abandon your daughter for seven years without a word? Without a single solitary freakin' word — and now that I've finally found someone, you finally decide to waltz back in?"

A single gasp is the only indication I have that my words are inflicting direct blows. I raise my eyes and look at the woman who was once my wife and when she establishes eye contact with me she says in a broken whisper, "You'll never know how much I regret my decision — but I can't take it back. Ketki is her own person without me. I can't explain what I did, she will never understand. Sometimes, I don't understand it myself, so how can I expect her to understand?"

"How can you help random people every day but not give a crap about your own daughter?" I ask, my lip curling in contempt.

"Don't you understand? That's why I went into nursing. I had to understand why I couldn't bond with my daughter. I felt like a defective human being. I wanted to know what was broken inside of me to explain why I didn't feel like a normal mom. I figured if I studied about it, I might understand what was wrong with me."

"Did you ever find any answers?" I ask almost sarcastically.

Tayanita shrugs as she answers, "Actually I did. Do you remember how volatile I was after Ketki was born? I probably had undiagnosed postpartum depression. When you combine that with Ketki's autism, it was like emotional TNT."

I can't keep the skepticism out of my glare as I probe, "Nita, our daughter is nine. So, where have you been all the rest of the years? I'm guessing you didn't suffer from postpartum depression all those years."

"No, I didn't. I *obviously* got treatment," she snaps defensively. "It took me a couple years to get on my feet. After I did, I remembered what all those doctors were telling us about Ketki — that she needed consistency and stability. If I had come rushing back in to your lives, I would've destroyed all you were trying to build with her."

I clear my throat uncomfortably.

"I know you, Mark, as soon as you had a solid diagnosis for Ketki, you would've been off and running — using as many types of therapy as you could possibly pack in. You are just that organized and practical. It was all I could do to get myself to work and back. I had worked so hard to get myself healthy and sane. I didn't want to upset everyone's applecart by trying to pretend I was some great mother when I didn't even have a clue. You are a better mom than I'll ever be."

"If what you say is true, you're not being fair to yourself. If you had postpartum depression, you don't even know what it's like to be Ketki's mom without having an impairment. How do you know you wouldn't be spectacular?"

"Don't do this to me, please," Tayanita pleads with tears spilling from the corners of her eyes. "I've had my chance with Ketki. I don't see any way to go back. She was too little when I left and I was too detached. She doesn't know me from a stranger in the line at the local warehouse store. It would be foolish and delusional for me to think otherwise. I don't know if my heart can handle the pain."

"Nita —" I interrupt.

She holds up her hand to stop me as she continues, "Mark, it's obvious Shelby loves your daughter to pieces — note I said *your* daughter — she is yours. I might be her mother biologically, but she is everything to *you*. Go on and build a family with Shelby. Don't hold out hope for me, I've got my own life. Be happy Mark."

"Tayanita, you know it's not that easy." I argue. "This isn't a game of SIMS, where Ketki can merely create another character if she wants a mom. *You* are her mom, whether I date Shelby or twenty other women, that doesn't change."

"Well, it seems as if Ketki hasn't suffered any by not having me around —" she replies defensively.

"How do you even know? You know nothing about her! You don't field all the questions she asks. You don't hear her when she talks about how she feels abandoned by not having a mother. You don't know anything! You can't make those assumptions. Do you want to know the honest truth? Our daughter thinks you hate her. She believes she wasn't good enough for you to stay around."

Tayanita sways in on the bench as she absorbs my words. "How could you tell her such terrible things about me?" she whispers hoarsely.

"Nita, I didn't tell her any of that stuff. She made it up to try to make sense of what happened. It didn't matter how many politically correct answers I gave her about why you left, she still made up a story line in her own head and it's the only one she will believe. It's probably the one she'll believe forever — unless you tell her the real truth."

"Are you sure Shelby didn't tell her that just to push me out of the picture? It doesn't seem like her, but some women will do that sort of stuff, you know," my ex-wife suggests skeptically.

"Good God no! I only started dating Shelby a few months ago. Ketki started with this schtick about you hating her around the time one of her teachers adopted her stepdaughter and brought a slideshow to school to show the ceremony. I think she was about five at the time. Since the little girl had two moms and Ketki didn't have any moms, the math didn't add up to her so she made all sorts of assumptions about why it happened. No amount of explanation from me made any difference."

"Mark, I'm so sorry. I guess I never considered how hard it would be to explain my absence. I figured since my brain somehow didn't operate correctly, you would be better off if I wasn't there somehow. In retrospect, it all sounds so selfish and weird, but I never intended it to be that way, I swear."

"Nita, I think deep down in my heart I knew that. That's why I don't hate you. Sometimes, I'm downright furious with you, but I never hated you for your decision."

Tayanita swallows hard. "Thank you."

"I have to be honest with you though, I don't know what route is the healthiest for Ketki. There is a part of her which believes wholeheartedly that the reason you're not in her life is because you hate her. I think she needs to know you don't. On the other hand, if you're planning to be in and out of her life, I don't know if that's good either."

"I don't know where I would fit in your world. I don't want to step on Shelby's toes."

"That's a whole other topic — What if Shelby doesn't get better? How will I break the news to Ketki?" I ask. "I would like forever with Shelby, but what if we don't have forever?"

"Mark, you can't think that way. You have to think in

terms of Shelby making it. You and I have had our shot and we didn't work out so well. We make great friends, but terrible life partners."

"There's a reason Shelby is in your life. Let's fight to keep her there."

CHAPTER THIRTEEN

SHELBY

SHELBY, WHY IS MY dad acting so weird? Is it because you're so sick? He wasn't acting this way the last time. Maybe it's because his trial got changed. Do you think that's it?"

By now, I should be used to Ketki's unorthodox pattern of speech bursts. This one, however, catches me off guard because I'm already lost in my thoughts and one of my medications is giving me a colossal headache. Her barrage of questions draws me up short though. Mark and I haven't had a chance to have a heart-to-heart conversation about what he wants her to know about her mom. If I answer any questions, I would be winging it and I'm not comfortable with that approach. I'm more of a "honesty is the best policy" kinda gal. Ketki has obviously picked up on the fact that her dad might not be in the same camp.

I try for the indirect approach. "Your dad hasn't been getting very much sleep because I've been miserable. I've been throwing up a lot and since I have incisions everywhere, it's next to impossible for me to get any sleep. I've been bugging him a bunch. Maybe he's just cranky because he's not used to having me around."

Ketki twirls her hair around her fingers and wrinkles her brow for several moments. "I don't think so. You were sick before, and he didn't act this way. Maybe it's about Uncle Callum. Dad's always in a weird mood when he goes to see the Jade lady. I think it has to do with the dream catcher on his back. Maybe he's catching bad thoughts in it instead of nice ones. I wish I could draw as good as Jade, because then Dad would smile more."

I've been half listening to Ketki's spontaneous barrage of words until her bizarre non sequitur catches my attention. I pivot my head until I'm looking directly at her and ask, "Wait. What did you say? What do you mean?"

"Remember when my aunt had to drop me off early because she had an appointment? Dad wasn't at work; he was visiting the Jade lady. When I was there, she was showing me how she used her tattoo-pokey machine to put color in the feathers on his back. That was the first time I saw Daddy smile in a while. Maybe if I could draw pictures instead of playing computer games, Dad would smile more at me. I wanted her to do one on me too, but she said she couldn't because I'm too little."

My heart crumbles in a million little pieces as I realize once again the airtight family unit Ketki and Mark really are. It breaks my heart to realize how much responsibility Ketki feels for Mark's well-being.

I pat the couch next to me so Ketki can sit down as I reply, "You know, I've watched you and your dad play games on the computer before. He smiles plenty when you guys play together."

Ketki's eyebrows raise in surprise. "I don't think you're telling me the truth. Daddy doesn't smile when we play computer games. He frowns a lot and then pretends not to say bad words."

I snicker at her response, the child does not miss much. Her answer is actually dead on. "I can't argue with you — because you're not wrong. Still, in between those times when you do something super complicated or something he can't do, he smiles and cheers for you like you would not believe. Your dad enjoys seeing you do well."

"*R-i-i-ight,*" Ketki replies dubiously. "So, I suppose that's why he calls me an ungrateful winner?"

"For the sake of peace, you could tone down your victory dance a tad. It can get a little obnoxious," I concede.

"Maybe we should send daddy on a staycation," she suggests.

I giggle as I respond, "A stay what?"

"On a stay-cation," Ketki answers confidently. "I saw it on one of those travel channels. It's a vacation where you stay home and do nothing. It would be like daddy went on a business trip. Whenever I ask him how he is after he goes away for work, he says he's 'absolutely fine and that the trip was super-duper relaxing'. If he has so much fun on a real business trip, he would have a really great time on a staycation where he didn't actually have to work."

I can't help but grin, because her logic makes me smile. Just out of curiosity, I ask her, "You've got your dad taken care of, but what will we do?"

"We'll have a slumber party, a'course." Ketki answers with a shrug. "My dad already said I could do it weeks and weeks ago — but you got too sick. I guess we'll have it in the summer instead."

"Hmm, it might make it tricky to invite your classmates," I remark.

"They wouldn't want to come anyway. Remember the birthday party?"

"How are you going to have a slumber party with no guests?" I ask, puzzled.

"I'm inviting you. Dad just said the people I invited had to go to school and be as nice as me. Since you're a teacher, you go to school."

I can't fault her logic. Unorthodox, yes. Wrong, no. "Thank you, Ki. But, it might be a quiet slumber party since I'm not up to getting up and dancing and having fun. Do you mind if I invite my new friends?"

Ketki is pensive for a moment. "Does my dad know these people? I think that's a rule too."

Doing a brief mental catalogue, I nod my head. "I think all my friends are students too. I'll check and make sure everyone is free. So, who is going to break it to your dad that he's not invited to this shindig — you or me?"

Ketki examines me closely. "Normally I would say you, but you look a little beat up. Maybe we shouldn't point that out to Dad right now. He might not let you have friends come over to play if he thinks you don't feel well. I'll handle this mission solo."

"Good strategy. I'll see about the rest of the crew. How does pizza and ice cream sound for the menu?"

"You're not planning to put anything yucky on it,

right?" Ketki clarifies.

"No yucky stuff allowed, this is going to be an epic slumber party!"

"Ketki, I have to say, you are a most excellent video game coach. When my brother was alive, he tried to teach me this game and it never worked because he was way too impatient with me. *Tetris* is way more fun than I ever remember. Thanks for teaching me," Jade compliments as she swings her bunny slippers up and down casually and leans back in the gaming chair.

"Is that why you're friends with Shelby? Shelby's brother died too. What happened to your brother?" Ketki asks abruptly.

I can tell Jade isn't prepared for the question as she visibly flinches, but she quickly recovers and responds, "I don't know exactly, but people who knew him said that a few guys were being really mean to him and it made him feel sad. He didn't know he had lots and lots of other friends, so he killed himself to get rid of the pain."

"Is it weird that your brother's dead?" Ketki blurts.

At first, Jade seems stunned, but then she lets out a gasp of air mixed with laughter as she admits, "Yeah. It is weird. It's *totally* weird. Even after all these years it's weird. I don't know if it's ever not going to be weird."

Hearing her say it out loud unlocks something inside me. "Oh thank goodness you said that. People look at me strange when I say I miss my brother because I was so young when I lost Owen. They think I should somehow forget what my life was like before he died — like I'm an Etch-a-Sketch machine or something. Just shake me up with a few court papers and my past suddenly doesn't matter."

"I hear where you're coming from," Jessica, one of Jade's friends says. "Even though I was adopted by my grandparents, everybody wants me to forget I knew my parents and could remember them fighting like cats and dogs in front of me."

Ketki is listening as the conversation unfolds like a complicated tennis match. Finally she makes a seemingly random observation, but I have a feeling it's profoundly enlightening for her.

"Wait a minute … so… *nobody* here has a normal family?" she asks softly.

The girl with fiery red hair, Jessica, shakes her head. "Nope. Eventually, I'm going to marry into a pretty normal family, but mine was anything but normal growing up. My mom couldn't decide whether she wanted to go or stay. I never knew whether I was important enough for her and my dad to stick around. Finally, the lure of the road became too much and they left me behind to be raised with my grandma and grandpa."

"Wow, that sounds like what happened with me and my dad. My mom decided she hated me too much to stick around, so she left. She didn't even say goodbye," Ketki muses sadly.

Rogue reaches out to place her arm around Ketki's shoulders. Ketki freezes in place but does not shrug off the contact. Rogue probably doesn't realize this, but that's a huge sign of progress in their relationship. It took me weeks before Ketki would allow me to get that close to her. Autism is a funny thing. It can create interesting boundaries.

"*Guerrerita*, you might think you understand everything your mom and dad were going through when they made those decisions," Rogue says. "However, I can almost guarantee you that you don't. I was once in your shoes. You know the older guy you met down at the shop … Isaac?"

Ketki nods her head solemnly. "He let me organize his coin collection."

"Well, that man is my dad. He's Ivy's dad too — but I didn't know him at all. I grew up thinking he deserted my mom and I for no reason. It turns out he was told something very different which changed everyone's lives. It wasn't anyone's fault; it just happened. So, until you know the whole story, you can't really judge your mom," Rogue advises.

"How am I supposed to talk to my mom when I don't know where she is? Maybe she was like me and somebody bullied her? What if she killed herself like Jade's brother or what if she got sick like Shelby? Maybe she died like Shelby's brother. How do I get answers then?" Ketki asks staring down the adults in the room.

I suddenly realize Ketki's pain and uncertainty goes far deeper than I knew. Fortunately, I know a person who can help provide her with more definitive answers — unfortunately, I'm not free to have that discussion with anyone yet.

I attempt to establish eye contact with Ketki as I try to clarify the situation without breaking any confidences, "Ketki, just because your mom and dad couldn't make it as a couple, it doesn't mean your mom didn't love you or anything bad happened to her. People get married too young or for the wrong reasons all the time. Sometimes, the grown-up decides to leave so they stop hurting the other person."

I am saved from a long drawn out conversation by the jangling sound of the doorbell. Ketki shrieks with delight. "The pizza is here! Now we can really party"

Jessica rolls her eyes. "Oh great! I am never, ever going to fit into my wedding dress."

"Did you bring your wedding dress *here*?" Ketki asks excitedly.

"Well, not here with me tonight," concedes Jessica, "but, I do have it here with me in Florida. I'm going to attend a young readers conference next week and I happened to find a dress I totally love while I was here. Mitch is probably not going to be real thrilled about carting it all over the country."

Ketki and I both exclaim, "Oh my gosh!" at the same time.

Jessica laughs in delight at our twin expressions. "Yes?" she inquires teasingly.

I defer to Ketki and allow her to go first because she is literally jumping up and down as she asks, "Can I help with your wedding? I always wanted to."

Jessica tilts her head and looks at Ketki. "You would look stunning with wildflowers braided in your hair. Let me check with my fiancé and make sure he doesn't already have a family member slated for this — but I'm sure you'd be a wonderful flower girl."

Ketki looks like someone told her the solar flares were a permanent condition on planet Earth. Her eyes are wide with shock and her mouth is wide open. Finally, she speaks, "Wait, I don't *want* to be a flower girl. There are way too many people and I don't wear dresses because they're itchy."

"I thought you said you wanted to help with Jess's wedding," Jade probes.

"*I do!*" Ketki insists. "I want to make one of those cool projection light shows for the wedding cake. I'd program it with my computer. It'd be like coding for a game. They look totally rad. I could put your names in them and everything."

Jessica gasps and puts her hand over her mouth as she starts to dance with excitement. "Are you serious? I saw those on one of those fancy cooking channels. I fell in love with the idea, but I knew it would never be in our budget. Mitch will be so jazzed. Do you think you could put a few dogs into the design?"

"2-D or 3-D?" responds Ketki with a look of concentration.

"Hey, you guys can come on down to Ink'd Deep and use the light box for the design if you want. It sounds like it might make it easier," Jade offers.

"Yeah, I've got new auto CAD software I had to buy for a class a couple terms ago which might help with that too," Ivy adds.

Jessica can barely hold back tears as she remarks, "I miss you guys so much. Kansas is nice and all, but you all are my family too."

"What's holding you in Kansas?" I ask, unfamiliar with Jessica's story.

"That's a good question, since we seem to spend most of our time on the plane headed here. The airlines have threatened to give our dogs their own frequent flyer cards. Even my grandparents aren't opposed to retiring here anymore. Mitch just built Hope's Haven and invested a bunch of money and getting training facilities up and running in Kansas though. It seems crazy to walk away."

"I don't think he's walking away," Rogue argues. "Your fiancé does an incredible amount of work with my husband. It's not like he's slacking off."

"It's true. It's almost as if Devon and Riley run the place on their own most of the time anyway."

"Well, there you go," Jade says with a note of finality. "Now can we get back to the fun part of the evening. I am dying to eat. Besides, I've got some new video game skills to conquer."

Abruptly, Jessica turns toward me. "Were you going to tell me something?"

I blush as I reply, "Yes, but my news isn't nearly as exciting as everyone else's. I was just going to tell you I think you are my team leader next week at the library. I'm going to the *Promoting the Power of Prose* training."

Jessica grins. "Oh, this will be so much fun. You've only seen the quiet side of me tonight. Wait until I perform in front of a crowd."

My heart pounds a little. I'm not sure if it's from fear or anticipation.

CHAPTER FOURTEEN

MARK

I TOSS MY DIRTY leather gloves into the back of Tristan's work truck and I try to brush off my pants before entering the restaurant. As Tristan and I are walking across the parking lot, I notice Declan, Marcus and a guy I was introduced to as Mitch walking toward us. When I see Marcus, I ask, "I never mind helping out on a Habitat for Humanity house, but I have a feeling there is something else going on. What's up?"

"Shelby is at a conference thing with Jess and Diamond, right?"

"Yeah. She doesn't start her next round of chemo for a couple weeks. Why?"

"Where is Ketki?" Tristan asks. Something in the tone of his question makes my stomach clench.

"My sister was brave and took Ki camping with her kids. Ketki without computer access ought to be interesting —"

Tristan smiles slightly. "If she's anything like me, she's probably just programming in her head and waiting until she can code it into the computer."

I shake my head in agreement. "You're probably right. But as you know, I'm not a big believer in coincidences, so I have to ask — why is everyone here?"

"You're right. It isn't a coincidence. My wife thought it would be a good idea for us to talk to you about Ketki. Since we're all together anyway, I decided to work on the latest Habit project. We've worked together often in the past and it's pretty seamless to get us together. By the way, you didn't tell me you have mad, ninja-like tiling skills. Way to hold out on me —"

"Another time I'll tell you about the summer I made my living restoring bathrooms in hotels, but right now I want you to tell me why my daughter is even almost the topic of our conversation?" I demand, feeling myself grow warm.

Declan steps forward when he hears the conversation heat up. "It's all good, really. Jade was in on this too. Remember last weekend when the girls sent us off to play laser tag and watch movies? It turns out they had a girls night too." We reach a back booth where the rest of the gang is already seated, but I can't help but feel like I'm getting ready to face down a firing squad. I have no idea what's about to happen.

Isaac pats the vinyl seat beside him. "Sit. It will all be better with food, I promise. I ordered the usual stuff."

Reluctantly I slide down into the seat next to Isaac. I like the guy, but there is something about his almost military bearing, which makes me feel like I'm being hauled into the principal's office whenever I speak to him. It's like speaking to an elder of our tribe.

"Am I going to need something stronger than Pepsi

for this meeting?" I ask, not entirely sure it's a joke.

"You know, this probably has become such a big deal simply because Jess is involved," Mitch admits.

Everyone around the table nods. Tristan interjects, "I suppose Ketki would relate to her the most."

I hold up my hands in a timeout gesture as I sharply whistle to stop the surrounding conversation. "Will somebody please start at the beginning of the story? Why is everyone suddenly so concerned about Ki? You've all known her for a few months now — well everyone except Mitch."

Tristan clears his throat before he responds, "I don't know if you know this about everyone in the group, but there isn't a simple story among us. My mom gave up a child for adoption as a young woman and later ended up raising her grandson after my sister passed away. Jade's brother committed suicide, and Jessica's parents essentially dropped her off at her grandparent's house and forgot to pick her up."

"Don't forget whatever craziness that happened with our wives —" interjects Marcus.

"Okay, that's interesting. But what does it all have to do with Ketki?" I push.

"It seems Ketki has some wild ideas about what might have happened to your ex-wife," Isaac answers shaking his head. "Ketki thinks her mother killed herself."

"What? That's crazy even for Ketki. I know for a fact Tayanita isn't dead. In one of the most bizarre incidences of 'I can't seem to bury my past', my ex-wife was actually taking care of the love of my life before I even knew about it."

Suitably amazed looks cross the faces around the table as Isaac asks, "Does Ketki know this?"

"Of course not! How do I go about telling Ketki her mom is alive, but isn't sure she wants to see her? I don't want to break my daughter's heart. That would be beyond cruel. It's almost worse than Ketki assuming Tayanita is dead."

"I don't know if it is." Isaac responds sagely. "Kids' minds can come up with some interesting ideas."

Marcus shakes his head. "I don't know what to tell you … I just know my wife is really concerned Ketki may be blaming herself for things she shouldn't even be worried about at her age. Maybe you can convince your ex-wife to talk to Ketki. Tell her what really happened — it can't be any worse than what Ketki's making up."

"I guess not," I concede. "I mean, Ketki has said a few odd things here and there, but I didn't think she thought about Tayanita much. Maybe having Shelby around has brought it all up to the surface."

Declan chuckles softly. "Yeah, I kind of learned the hard way. For every good thing which happens in your life, there's always a downside. You have to remember that when you're dealing with the down side not to forget there is a good side."

Declan's advice is as random as heck, but it's not incorrect. Even though Shelby's presence in our little home has been fraught with all sorts of complications, Ketki and I have never been happier.

"Just once, I'd like all the stuff we have to deal with to be not quite so complicated." I heave a heavy sigh.

"As Jessie's grandfather once told me, it's the complications which make life worth it — otherwise we'd be bored to tears."

"Cancer and breaking my daughter's heart both suck big time. Given my choice, I'd settle for boring," I reply, settling back in the booth.

This is the first time I've been inside the offices of Identity Bank, but the operation looks incredibly impressive.

"Hey, I'm sorry for having to call you into a meeting here, but I've got some new equipment being delivered today and I need to be on hand when it arrives," Tristan looks up from his big executive desk.

It's weird for me to see him in this environment — usually I see him in a collegiate sweatshirt and torn jeans. I forget he is a corporate entity all on his own. Today, he looks every bit like a Fortune 100 Rising Star executive he is. "It's not a problem. I've got a little free time before I'm scheduled to give a deposition anyway and it's just up the street. I find if I get too wound up over them, I start to ask stupid questions. Speaking of stupid questions, why am I here?" I ask.

"You and I had an informal discussion a while back about Shelby's family. How serious are you about following up?"

"It depends. Will it hurt Shel?" My head spins with the potential ramifications.

"I don't know. Like I said before, it's hard to predict how these things will go. This would be limited exposure, because the only person I have located so far, is her sister,

Savannah."

"Really? Where does she live? What does she do?" I rattle off questions as fast as they hit my brain.

Tristan's eyebrow hitches up. "Easy there, Counselor. Last I checked, I'm not a hostile witness."

I force myself to ease back in my chair as I wait for him to answer my questions. "You're right. I guess I'm just anxious to bring Shelby some good news for a change."

"I understand. I met my wife on one of these reunions. I know they can be emotional. We almost missed this one altogether because of an interesting little coincidence which threw our search engines off. It's a good thing I've got practicum students who go through each search and confirm the results by hand."

I lean forward in my chair as I warn, "Macklin, I'm a patient man, but I'm not that patient."

"Okay, moving on …" Tristan continues, chuckling.

He pulls a file from the pile in front of him and starts to leaf through some papers as he says to himself, "I can't get over the city name. One, Savannah Georgina Lyons, is currently residing in Savannah, Georgia. It appears Savannah was born to Nancy and George Lyons on February 23, 1983."

An involuntary chill goes up the back of my spine as I realize we are ridiculously close to the point of no return, and Shelby doesn't even realize I've begun the journey. Tristan removes a piece of paper from the file and hands it over. "I can see what you mean about the formatting. That's a good catch. I wonder if she chose her location for subterfuge?" I ponder.

"That idea occurred to us at Identity Bank as well.

Yet, everything else she does on a daily basis is far out in the open. She runs a little paint-yourself-a-work-of-art shop in a trendy neighborhood. Unlike her parents, she doesn't seem to exactly be living in hiding."

"I wish I could stick her in a jury box and ask her some *voir dire* questions —" I muse.

Tristan laughs at my suggestion but offers one of his own, "Listen, I've learned the hard way that these transitions seem to go better if I'm around to answer questions in person. I'm driving up to Savannah to meet with her tomorrow. Do you want to ride along so you can get some eyeballs on her to make yourself feel better? Just to be clear, I'm not giving you permission to give her an interrogation or put her under oath. I just thought you might want to see how her demeanor strikes you."

I pull out my phone and check my appointments. "I have an eight thirty appointment tomorrow for twenty minutes. This guy is a bit of a talker, so it might be thirty. I'm free after that. Savannah's what … four hours away?"

"Give or take depending on traffic. Oh, Littleson — don't be a dick. It tends to work better if you're a not a jerk."

"I'll give it my best shot."

"You do that. There could be a lot at stake," Tristan says with a sigh.

The neighborhood where Paint Your Art Out is located is similar to the vibe where Ink'd Deep and Frannie's are in Gainesville. It's a mix of cool, new and retro. I did a contract negotiation on a start-up where they specialized in creating memory books. I remember being astonished by the sheer number of customers who participated in that kind of activity. *Shelby's sister must do pretty well to afford rent in this neighborhood* I think to myself as Tristan and I head through the front door.

A tall, graceful woman with a riotous head of reddish, blond curls, wearing a brightly colored apron greets us with a wide smile. "Hello, welcome to Paint Your Art Out. How can I help you this morning?"

People often claim I'm a little intimidating, so I make a conscious effort to be pleasant. "Good morning. Cool place you have here."

As soon as I speak, the smile slides off of Savannah's face. She sighs as she turns on her heel. "I was hoping for actual customers today, but I'll get you copies of the paperwork," she remarks over her shoulder as she starts to leave the room.

"Ma'am, why *do* you think we're here?" Tristan inquires.

Savannah's eyes roll so hard I half expect them to make a noise like a one armed bandit at a casino.

"I was suspicious before, but with a question like that, now I'm positive you're not here to be craftsy. If I were to venture a guess, I would say you," she says pointing at Tristan, "are some sort of law enforcement." She swings her finger toward me and remarks, "You're a little harder to figure out. I can't decide if you're here to sell me legal insurance or if you're actually one of the ambulance-chasers yourself."

Tristan lets out a low whistle of admiration. "I am impressed. I could use you on my team."

"Team of what?" Savannah asks suspiciously. "I'm sorry to say, but you guys don't look like any of the building inspectors who have come around lately."

I flash her a tight grin. "That's because we're not."

Tristan steps forward and hands Savannah a business card. "Ma'am, I'm here on a bit of personal mission today. It's even more personal for Mr. Littleson here. However, if you don't want him present, I understand. He can go if you would prefer."

Savannah takes a moment to scrutinize the business card. She looks up at Tristan. "Wait a minute. *Identity Bank.* You guys were on the news about that huge catfishing story. I'm not involved in any cat fishing. Aren't you like filthy rich and worth more money than Mark Cuban? I thought I read somewhere that you asked your girlfriend to marry you by kidnapping her on a plane?"

"That is my company. I am Tristan Macklin. I did ask my wife, Rogue, to marry me on a trip to Paris although the details can get a little twisted depending on who's telling it," Tristan confirms.

"Umm… I don't know what you're doing with my little company. All my paperwork is in order. That's what I was trying to tell you when you first came in," Savannah explains. Her anxiety level seems to be climbing with every word.

Tristan's voice drops as he attempts to clarify again, "Hunting down identity thieves is not the only thing my company does. We also do adoption reunificat —"

Tristan doesn't even get the whole word out of his mouth before Savannah gasps and holds a trembling hand over her mouth. "You mean you're here about Shel?"

Tristan and I nod carefully as Savannah peaks around us to find Shelby.

"Well, where is she?" Savannah demands. "I want to see my baby sister. I don't understand."

"Ma'am if you'll let me —" Tristan tries to redirect.

Savannah paces before she comes to a dead stop and slumps against a wall. "Please don't. *Oh please don't* tell me another one is dead," she pleads with alarm. "I tried to tell them I was old enough to take Shelby, but they wouldn't listen," Savannah half-mutters as she aimlessly walks in a circle around the store.

I catch Tristan's line of sight over Savannah's head and we seem to develop a plan of action without speaking. Since I'm closest to Savannah, I guide her toward some couches in the back of the store while Tristan locks the front door and hangs up the closed sign. Once I find the refrigerator and retrieve some cold water, Savannah objects. "It's been a slow month. I can't afford to close."

"This is entirely my fault. I should've timed things better. Sell me whatever equals double your daily sales. In fact, I might just buy enough to put some inventory in the Elliott Houses we are opening here and in Kansas," Tristan pledges.

Savannah narrows her gaze as she looks sideways at Tristan, "I know it doesn't look like it right now, but I don't need your charity. Usually my store does pretty well. The weather's been really strange and people haven't been coming out — but usually I do okay. I'll be fine."

"Look, it's my screw-up and I don't want to cost you a day's business — just think of me as a regular customer on a bigger scale," Tristan argues.

Finally, Savannah slumps against the back of the couch. "Fine, your money is as green as the next person's.

I'm not in any position to turn away cash at this point. Besides, we have more important things to talk about."

I nod. "We do."

"Why do you all look as if you're about to march in front of a firing squad when you talk about her? What the heck is going on? Did she turn into a serial killer or something?"

I laugh at the absurdity of the thought. "No, nothing could be further from the truth. Your sister is phenomenal. My daughter absolutely loves her and I'm not far behind. Her kind spirit and generosity is one of the first things that grabbed my attention about her," I gush.

"That's nice, but there's something you're not telling me —" Savannah intuitively guesses.

I try to find the words to coherently answer her question, but inexplicably even though I make my living with words, I can't seem to find them at the moment. Tristan seems to sense my dilemma as he solemnly looks at Savannah and proceeds to break her heart, one word at a time.

Chapter Fifteen

Shelby

"Remind me why I'm doing this for you again? I already graduated from college. I was supposed to be done with term papers, remember?" I grouse as I help Rogue format her bibliography.

"Only because you're the best friend in the whole wide universe and I owe you a lifetime supply of fancy coffee ..." Rogue answers as she sorts her flashcards. "I'm so sorry. I don't know why this paper snuck by me on the syllabus. Usually I'm much more on top of things."

"Why isn't your husband helping with all of this?" I ask. "Isn't he some sort of computer guru with magical tools to suck thoughts right out of your brain?"

Rogue sighs wistfully. "I wish. He's actually on a high priority project with your hunk at the moment. I didn't have a great connection with him, but it sounded like he said something about making families whole or something like that. Anyway, it sounded like something pretty positive. He rarely gets too hyped about anything specific, but he seemed very excited."

Rogue's words echo in my mind like a sick

soundtrack. If I'm honest with myself, I knew this was a possibility ever since that weird day at the hospital when we came face-to-face with Tayanita and I discovered who she was. Yet, somehow I assumed I would actually be involved in the ending of our relationship. It's funny, I thought after all we been through, Mark would fight harder for us.

Maybe I'm being unfair. After all, Tayanita had him first. She is Ketki's mom and they are the original family. There is a lot to be said for Ketki feeling grounded and whole. Just as loudly, my less charitable side argues Tayanita had her chance once and gave it up. What about the fact that Ketki loves and trusts me? Why should Ketki have to give me up simply because her 'real mom' is back in her life and wants a second shot?

A wave of nausea overtakes me. It's too strong for even the industrial-strength anti-nausea medicines the doctors have me on to combat my chemotherapy regimen. I have to leap up and run toward the restroom to throw up.

When I return, Rogue exclaims, "*¡Dios mío!* You look like you've had a come-to-Jesus moment and seen a ghost all at once. What happened?"

Well, maybe not a ghost but close enough. "You know, I haven't been in a lot of relationships, but I sort of thought there would be a dramatic fight at the end. After all we've been through with the melanoma, I didn't figure Mark would just walk away because his ex-wife showed up. I am trying to be the bigger person here for Ketki, but I'm not feeling very big. I'm feeling like the old family hound who got kicked out on the back porch for the new shiny puppy,"

"Are you sure you're interpreting this correctly?"

Rogue cautions. "I don't know Mark well — but he strikes me as very much the same kind of man as my husband. The kind of man who sees life like a gigantic chessboard and who doesn't make moves without a great deal of thought and consideration of those around him. In all the months I've seen Mark interacting with you, he's done nothing which wasn't to benefit you — even if he was clumsy and awkward and pushy as all heck."

I stop to think about her point for a moment. "Okay, that's true. But he's never had to balance me against his ex-wife before. What if there are still latent feelings there? Is it better for Ketki in the long run for them to be together because I'm so sick? What if it's better for Mark for them to stay a family?" I speculate. "You saw how broken up Ketki is about her mom. Maybe being reunited is the best thing for them. Perhaps I should just step out of the way."

"Hold up!" Rogue interrupts. "You don't know any of this to be a fact. I thought you talked to Mark about this. Didn't he say they were merely childhood friends who married in a rush? Why are you in a hurry to give them a happily ever after ending they never had in the first place?"

Rogue's words bring me up short. That's an excellent question. Why am I so quick to give away my own happily-ever-after? Even though I'm sick from my chemotherapy and my other medications and I struggle against a multitude of side effects from extreme itchiness, puffiness and nausea, I have never been happier. An interesting thing is happening to me as I look at myself through Mark's eyes. Even though I have deep ugly incisions and scabs where there used to be none, he makes me feel beautiful and cherished. At a time when the world defines me as ugly, Mark not only says I am stunning, he routinely shows me how he feels. Am I really willing to walk away from all of this just because it might be convenient for another family? I don't have to dig very deep for the answer. Every cell in my body screams no. I have found my happy. I'm not so quick to give it up. I just have to figure out this cancer stuff and get it under control.

I roll my shoulders and grab some Kleenex off of the desk as I dry my eyes and blow my nose. "Come on Rogue, *French Impressionist Artists of the Twentieth Century* won't organize themselves. I'll deal with all the rest of the stuff later. I can't sort it out without Mark here anyway."

I surreptitiously check my phone after the nurse finishes checking my vitals. I don't understand why Mark isn't here yet. He told me he would be here twenty minutes ago. He's been acting beyond bizarre recently. I can't help but wonder if this is just a form of slow-motion breakup. Finally, my phone vibrates and I see a text.

No texting, but juror passed out in court Judge held us. So sorry I won't be there. Can you pick up Ketki?

My shoulders slump in relief. At least there's an explanation. There's a knock on the door and Dr. Charleston comes in and sits behind the consulting desk and puts my most recent PET scans up on the display board. While he's arranging things, I quickly type an affirmative answer to Mark and put my phone away.

"All by yourself today?" Dr. Charleston asks as he leafs through my file.

"Apparently, Mark is stuck in court today." I shrug.

"I've seen him in action. He is a very impressive fellow," the doctor remarks with a grin.

I smile. "I think so, but I might be biased."

Dr. Charleston turns on a huge overhead light. "Ms. Lyons, come on over here let's take a look."

I'm not particularly shy about my body. You can't grow up under the conditions I did and be overly modest. But there is something distinctly different about this strip-down. The stakes feel so high. I clutch my hospital type gown around me and it feels dozens of sizes too large as I stand under the lamp. The heat from the lamp feels reminiscent of the tanning beds I used to use as a teenager. It's hard not to feel a moment of would've, should've and could'ves. If only I had made different choices or been more aware, maybe I wouldn't be standing under this lamp having a doctor look at me with a magnifying glass in his hand with an intense expression on his face. The longer we stand there, the more nervous I become.

It gets a bit awkward when I have to move my breast for him to see one particularly ugly scar. This one doesn't seem to want to heal correctly. He examines my wound closely. "Is this the area the first physician tried to scrape in the office?"

I nod carefully. "Unfortunately, yes. That was not a pleasant experience. It's a good thing she didn't warn me in advance she was planning to do it or I would've climbed the walls. It hurt!"

Dr. Charleston nods sympathetically. "I imagine it did. Unfortunately, her hasty decision to treat you without having diagnostics has compromised that site and made healing more difficult in a couple of areas. Overall, I'm pleased with how well you're healing and how well you've responded to outpatient chemo. However, there are a couple of troublesome areas where we may have to develop a different protocol for treatment."

"What does that mean exactly?" I ask with trepidation.

"Well, we need to see how the genetic analysis comes back on your samples — I'm going to send you to a bigger facility so you can have targeted gene therapy and other more cutting-edge procedures done that we simply don't offer in this small setting."

My heart absolutely sinks — but I put on a brave face and smile as I say, "You know me, I'm like a child of the wind. I'm adaptable."

Dr. Charleston smiles a kindly grin. "I wish all of my patients had such a flexible attitude. It will take you far Ms. Lyons. I'll have my PA contact you with more details once we know more. I'm glad I got a chance to see you again, although I am sorry it had to be this way."

I had to register for school today and you and Dad weren't there," Ketki announces as soon as she gets into my car.

"I'm sorry. I had no idea. I thought you were already registered." I back out of the parking space.

"Most kids are, but they kicked a few kids out of the system because of our first names. Apparently they think my first name is one big typo. I don't know how come they think that because I've had the same first name since I was in preschool. It's not even like I changed it. I guess they don't respect the fact that I have a Native American name. I don't understand why I have a Cherokee name and my dad doesn't have one. It makes no sense. He says his parents gave him a non-Native name because there was a missionary in their village who saved my grandpa's life when he was a teenager and they gave my dad his name as a big thank you for what he'd done. Still, don't you think it's funny to have all these Cherokee names and then have an American name stuck right in the middle? I think it's hilarious."

I smile as her hands fly in active animation. "You're right, I've always wondered about the story behind your dad's name. I think your name is beautiful. I think everybody has weird ideas about their name. My name sounds like a country music song. Shelby Lynne Lyons."

Ketki giggles as she replies, "It totally does. Do you sing?"

I poke my bottom lip out in an exaggerated pout. "Nope. Not a single, solitary note. I was in math club and chess club, not choir."

"I thought the kids were trying to make you into one of the popular kids after you were adopted?" Ketki asks with a puzzled expression.

"Oh, they were in the beginning," I explain, "but, it didn't take them too long to figure out I was a lost cause. I hadn't gone to school with other kids. My sister Savannah was older than me, so when my mom and dad weren't paying any attention, she tried to play school with me and teach me stuff she remembered from when she used to go to school. It was easier for her to teach me math concepts because she didn't have to have books and writing stuff around. She could do it with things that she found in the environment. A lot of times she'd teach me math concepts when we were doing other things like laundry or cooking. I don't think she truly understood what a great teacher she was. She taught me very complicated stuff like how to add and subtract fractions and even how to multiply and divide them without having the luxury of pencils and paper or calculators. She taught me a little about music too from the old hymn books at the churches we would visit."

"I don't get it … why would your parents not want you to go to school?" Ketki asks. "I don't think I've ever heard of that before."

"I don't know the answer. I was very young when all this happened I wasn't much older than you are now. I was trying to figure it all out in my head and I was trying to take care of my little brother, who was very sick. We didn't have a permanent home like you have. We moved all the time. Savannah and I spent a lot of time worrying about how to stay warm and fed. My parents didn't trust a lot of people. When they did trust people, they always seemed to choose the wrong kind of people to trust."

"Maybe they were crazy. You know, some people say being autistic like me means you're crazy. I don't think that's true, but several of the mean people at school say so." She fiddles with her seatbelt.

Her simple declaration sears my heart. Even though we're only a couple miles from home, I pull into a strip mall and find a little ice cream shop. I count my lucky stars when I realize it's one of Ketki's favorite chains. As I help her unbuckle her seat belt and take her hand to walk across the parking lot, I am suddenly very grateful for a college degree in special education, which will help me explain to this phenomenally talented young woman why she is not only not crazy but may someday change the world. The only people crazy in this scenario are the one's trying to hurt Ketki.

When Mark suggested that perhaps I was brought into his life for a reason, I don't think this is what he had in mind, but I am honored to play this role if it helps a little girl believe in her potential.

Chapter Sixteen

Mark

As I throw my briefcase on the long L-shaped bench in the quiet homey-restaurant, I reflexively loosen my tie. I have to carefully bite my tongue before formulating an appropriate greeting for my ex-wife. After all, I did call this meeting. It's not Tayanita's fault Treadwell was able to land first chair in this trial. In my opinion, he not only needs to stay light years away from this trial, but from *any* trial. Sadly, my opinion doesn't seem to count for squat any more. Some days, I wonder why I even bother to try.

Tayanita doesn't say much as she watches me settle into the booth. Still, I feel compelled to apologize, "Sorry, it's just been one of those —"

"Mark, it's lunchtime. Eat." She points to the food in front of me. "It's not quite like we eat back home, but it's pretty close. I still miss fry bread. As soul cooking becomes more popular, it's a little easier to find savory bread pudding, but it's still not your mom's cooking."

I look down at the plates and I'm surprised to see a collection of my favorite foods. I was so preoccupied by the rest of my day, I didn't even notice the overflowing plates of food. "You didn't have to do this. How long have you been waiting?" I ask, suddenly embarrassed by her efficiency and my ineptness.

"Look, it's been years, but your tendency to cram ten things into the amount of time in which you probably should've done three isn't something you likely outgrew in your old age," Tayanita teases.

"I should probably take offense, but I'm the one who was late. So, I don't have much room to talk. I swear, in this case it wasn't my fault. I have a person in my office who, unfortunately, I have to call a 'colleague'. He is making my job very difficult. I spent an inordinate amount of time cleaning up after his sloppy mess this morning on redirect. He did such a piss-poor job on direct even the judge was confused."

Tayanita shoots me a sympathetic look as she responds, "Aren't you senior partner? Can't you do something about this guy?"

I shrug. "Allegedly, I am supposed to be doing something about it. I'm mentoring him. Unfortunately, he doesn't seem to be listening to any of the guidance I'm giving him. In fact, if I give him advice he seems to do exactly the opposite of what I tell him. It's absolutely infuriating."

"What do Susan and Jake say?" Tayanita asks.

It's all I can do not to break down into a completely inappropriate fit of laughter. This reminds me so much of when Tayanita and I would strategize throughout law school. We were always friends and partners first — before the colossal mess that was autism and presumably postpartum depression. I struggle to focus on her question as I answer, "Well, Jake has unofficially declared himself on a mental-health break, because he and

Charlesse broke up and are in the middle of a divorce. The man has a decent-sized divorce practice, but you would think he's the only person on earth to ever experience divorce. He's on his eighth month of this. Many women have babies faster than he's processing his emotional grief over it all."

Tayanita's jaw drops toward the ground at the bitterness in my tone. "Wow, way to be a sympathetic friend there," she replies sarcastically.

"Oh, my sympathy ended around the time he brought girls around the office who were barely older than Ketki to make him feel better about leaving his wife," I explain, wrinkling my nose in displeasure.

"Consider him off my Christmas card list," Tayanita comments sardonically.

"Are you kidding me? You didn't talk to me for more than half a decade, but you send my partners Christmas cards? What in the heck—"

"Hold on, *Unaduti.* You don't have a lot of room to talk. I've had the same PO Box since I started applying to colleges — it never changed. Where are my letters from you? The only letter I ever got from you was the divorce papers. Last I checked, communication goes both ways. You've known how to get a hold of me too. Before you go and play the martyr about how awful it was that I left you and Ketki — remember, you allowed yourself to be left. You knew where to reach me. I had the most obvious disappearance on the planet. I went to school in the same town, we had the same friends, our families stayed in close touch — Heck, we even use the same pharmacist. For the longest time I knew every time Ketki had an ear infection because he would tell me on the sly so I wouldn't worry. Of course, he didn't know he broke my heart with every update."

Feeling cornered, I lash out viciously, "So you're telling me you don't have any idea why Sid did that?"

Tayanita merely blinks at me with a crushed expression on her face. Her reaction should've been enough to stop me, yet somehow it's not.

"I'll tell you why he told you all that stuff. He assumed you would care — that you would be like a normal mom and give a crap. He never guessed you would abandon your daughter — y*our disabled daughter*. Do you get that? Do you know how much she struggles every single flippin' day?"

She just looks at me as if I have slapped her and in a way, I suppose I have. She takes her time as she stacks the plates carefully and moves them out of the way before she leans forward and looks directly in my face. She gets about six inches away from me before she says in a low, lethal voice "Of course I do. I am *a nurse*. A highly trained nurse with many specialties."

"Then how in the world could you up and walk away?" I accuse. "How could you leave — knowing what she would need from her parents — as in two parents? How did you just go on with your life?"

Tayanita whips her hair around and pops it back in a bun using a pen to hold it into place. "Look, I don't know what you want from me Mark, I thought I explained all this before. You acted like you understood where I was coming from, so what is this all about?"

My anger is taking me a little by surprise too. I'm not really sure how to answer. I thought I had worked through all of this years ago. Actually, I wasn't even sure I was terribly upset about it. I spent so many years telling people lies. I tried to pretend I wasn't devastated by the fact that Tayanita had simply walked away from our marriage and her daughter. I guess I believed my own hype. Clearly I'm a lot more pissed off than I'm willing to admit.

I shove a few bites of food in my mouth, but I couldn't tell you what I'm eating. It's just a stalling technique until I can bring my chaotic thoughts and emotions under a bit of control. Right now, I can't blame Tayanita for not being able to make sense of what I'm doing or saying, because even I can't untangle my thoughts.

Finally, I set the fork down and face her again. "I thought we had things under control too, but that was before our daughter started telling everyone she thought you hated her enough to kill yourself to avoid being in a relationship with her."

For that instant all animosity toward Tayanita dissipates as I watch her visceral reaction to my words.

"Do you suppose she *knows*?"

"Knows what?" I parrot, having completely lost track of the flow of the conversation.

"Maybe she doesn't know, because even you weren't aware. There was a time right before I left when I was sure if something didn't change I was going to hurt myself or Ketki, in the process. Things were that mixed up in my world," Tayanita admits as she tears a napkin in front of her up into small little pieces.

"Nita, you *never* said a word about that!" I exclaim. "You made it sound like you were just tired of the whole motherhood gig. My God! If I had known things were so bad, we could have done things so much differently. I'm sorry I didn't have any sympathy for you because I was exhausted too, I was in law school and trying to study for the bar. I thought you were simply whining over dirty diapers. I didn't have any idea you had any of that stuff going on. Nita, I had no idea you were planning to hurt yourself or Ki."

"All of that is why I *couldn't* tell you what was going on. You didn't need one more thing to juggle. I didn't know what was happening to me. I thought I was going absolutely crazy. Nobody I knew had an adverse reaction to babies All the people I saw on TV and in the movies who acted like I did were certifiably insane. I thought that's what was happening to me. I was going completely crazy for no reason. I had friends like this in high school who lost their minds, but they were using drugs and alcohol."

"Nita, I knew you weren't doing any of that crap — you're too smart."

Tayanita continues as if I didn't speak, "I wasn't drinking or doing drugs because I was at least trying to breast-feed Ketki. I felt like an abysmal failure as a mother because I couldn't breast-feed well. My child hated me and cried all the time and then I cried because my child cried — it just went on and on. I was supposed to love this motherhood thing and all it did was make me feel like I couldn't breathe or swallow or move. I felt paralyzed. Stuck. I couldn't help me, I couldn't help you, and I sure as heck couldn't help Ketki. I felt if I stayed one more second, I would put us all in grave danger."

Tayanita's words stop me cold. I realize instead of being angry at her, I should be grateful she left instead of hurting herself or Ketki. I've personally led civil cases against mothers for wrongful death. It's humbling to realize I could've been sitting in a completely different chair right now. We could've been facing each other in a courtroom — had she not made a safe choice.

"I didn't say this before, I guess I was too busy being a jerk before, but I'll say it now. Thank you."

A pained look crosses Tayanita's face. She holds up her hand to stop me. "Mark, no."

"No, I mean it. You made an incredibly brave, mature decision under extremely hard circumstances. I was giving you absolutely no support when I should've been. You deserve credit for making an impossible choice."

"Mark, I don't deserve credit for a decision I'm not sure I'd make again. Don't you get it? I regret my decision every other minute. I try not to even think about it, I try to pretend like I never had a daughter. How awful does that make me? I can't watch television because there are diaper commercials, Disney World commercials and commercials for IHOP and car rentals. Do you even know how many stupid items they advertise using children? It's thrown in my face everywhere I turn —"

I can feel Tayanita's anxiety in the pit of my stomach. She doesn't deserve this much pain. We may not have been the perfect star matched lovers, but we were always really great friends and it hurts me to see her in pain.

"Nita, Ketki is still your daughter. She's not dead. She lives less than an hour from you. She is smart, funny and laughs just like you. It might be better for both of you if you reintroduce yourself," I suggest quietly.

"What if she hates me?" Tayanita asks me with fear dripping from every syllable.

"I don't think that's possible. Ketki really wants you in her life. I believe she misses you. If nothing else, she's very curious about you and has a lot of questions."

"How do I even begin to answer those questions?" my former wife frets.

"With Ketki, there is only one approach which works. Complete and total honesty. She has a way of seeing through everything else like a laser guided missile," I caution.

"Really? You think I should tell her the whole story?"

"An age-appropriate version of it? Absolutely. She needs to understand you didn't just leave because you thought motherhood was a bad deal," I reply.

"What does Shelby think about me being back?" Tayanita scoops up all the pieces of napkin she's left on the table.

"She's fine with it," I answer confidently. "She wants to do whatever is best for Ketki."

Tayanita shakes her head and looks at me with an expression of pity. "Mark, you know that I'm saying this for your own good, not because I have any misguided idea there might someday be another chance for us, right?"

I chuckle softly. "I think everyone on the planet knows our ship sailed a long time ago and there are no more boarding passes. You were right to call me *Unaduti* — I was wool-headed."

"I want to make sure Shelby knows there isn't anything between you and me. There won't be, even if I come back. If I decide to do this, it's only because I never stopped loving Ketki and I don't want her to think something awful happened to me."

"You know, a lot of guys hate their ex-wives but you

keep doing these decent, heroic things which make it terribly hard for me to hate you. Bizarrely, I'm inclined to give you a hug right now, which is pretty surprising since a few minutes ago I was ready to scream at you."

"Trust me Mr. Hotshot Lawyer, you weren't the only one," Tayanita replies candidly.

CHAPTER SEVENTEEN

SHELBY

THE SECOND WEEK OF school used to always be my favorite week of the year. By then, everyone has settled down, learned everyone's name and is looking forward to everything new. The possibilities are limitless. I'll never forget my first year of school after I was removed from my parents. I felt like the world had been given to me on a platter. There were so many new worlds open — I never even knew they existed. Classes like science, social studies and language arts were mind-blowing. I thought new textbooks were some mystical gifts from the gods. Come to think of it, not much has changed. New books still fascinate me.

As I sip my hot apple cider and curl up with a mystery-romance novel, which under any other circumstances would probably be truly gripping, I can't help but mourn the loss of my dreams for this year. I can't set foot in the classroom this year. I can't really go anywhere. The chemotherapy has made me susceptible to random germs. The oncologists don't want me to be around a bunch of children. My new restrictions have even curtailed my volunteer work with Diamond at the library. It's like one crushing blow after another.

Just when I think I've got a handle on how much my life will be messed up by a few bad decisions I made as a teenager, Karma comes roaring back to remind me what a fool I was. I can't even tell you how disappointed I am. Jessica, Diamond and I were so pumped up after the *Promoting the Power of Prose* training. I was ready to steer my life in a new direction and apply my degree and love of reading and writing to a new setting. Once again, my life seems to have come unraveled like a sweater from a rummage sale.

I like Dr. Charleston, I really do. Yet, sometimes I wish he was a little less honest. No, I take it back. I don't wish that. Sometimes, his honesty hurts me to my core. When I started this journey, I hoped it would simply be a matter of taking a few bad skin cells off. As time has marched on, they just keep digging deeper and deeper. I feel like my body is a battle zone. Although I tried to tell myself that I was prepared for the worst, when Doctor Charleston told me I would need chemotherapy because the cancer had spread to my lymph nodes, I was not prepared for the blow. I'm not even thirty. How can I be dying from cancer? I did none of the risky behavior I associate with cancer. I don't smoke, I never took drugs. I stayed away from all the food with preservatives and food coloring. I don't touch food with artificial sweetener… much. Okay, so, I'll admit I'm a little addicted to Diet Mountain Dew, but I had to go to school and work at the same time. It's pretty much my only vice.

"The Dew" is my only vice unless you count Mark. It turns out that dark, witty, deeply spiritual barristers are my new vice. I take a break from my mini-pity party to eat one of the tiny quiches Mark served me for breakfast. When I mentioned I loved these little delicacies from a bakery across town, but one spice was making me sick since I started chemotherapy, Mark contacted the owner of the bakery and asked her if she'd make some just for me without the spice. She readily agreed and I now have my own supply of Shelby's Sublime Quiches. I did not expect her to add it to her menu and give a donation to the Skin Cancer Foundation in my name. It was such an incredibly sweet gesture from a complete stranger. I have a hard time wrapping my brain around it. Yet, that seems to sum up my whole existence the last few months, almost perfect strangers have gone out of their way to help make my life better.

I often wonder how many of the recent "miracles" in my life are due to random fate and how many of them are a result of the efforts of Mark Littleson. Sometimes, I think my man can move mountains. I swear — if he could take the cancer on himself, he would. He's a force of nature. I've never seen anything like it.

At first I thought he was like Reverend Frachett, but now I'm not so sure. I don't think the two men have much in common at all. Reverend Frachett was big on making empty promises and delivering very little. Mark doesn't say much about what he's planning to do, he's simply there when I need him.

I don't know what to do with myself. I feel twitchy. I can't seem to settle properly anymore. It's almost as if the cancer has made me hyper aware of every cell in my body. Some days, it seems even my hair hurts. So far, I've managed to keep most of my hair. It's a little thinner than it was, but it's there. I don't know why I've become so invested in keeping it, because I'm not a big fan of my hair. I've always hated its color and kinky, curly texture. Yet, somewhere along the way my battle to keep my hair has become symbolic of my battle to be victorious over cancer. I've tried every trick I've read about on the Internet. I wash my hair in cold water and even ice my scalp down when I take my chemotherapy treatments.

I even went as far as getting a prescription medication for hair growth. Dr. Charleston told me the evidence is mixed about whether it actually helps, but he was willing to allow me to try it. The whole thing is simply a stupid matter of pride. Yet, it doesn't stop me from fighting the battle. I don't know why it's become such a focal point for me. Maybe it's just easier to focus my attention on a minuscule, scalable problem that I can tangibly define, rather than the uncertain prognosis of my cancer. I don't know. At any rate, I appear to be winning the fight to keep my hair — or at least that's what my analysis of my hairbrush allows me to believe. It's one small positive in a wasteland of negatives so, I take a moment to celebrate.

I'm holding my hair up in pretend hairstyles and vogueing in front of the mirror while I sing along to Pink with absolutely no filter. I wasn't kidding when I told Ketki I have no singing skill. The key to having fun at this is wearing high-quality earphones and having the volume turned up really high. It works pretty well; I can't hear my own wretched singing.

When the song ends, I jump about three inches in the air when I suddenly hear clapping erupt from behind my left ear. I spin around on my heel, but trip over the laundry basket of clothes I was folding and end up in Mark's arms as he reaches out to catch me.

As he steadies me and helps me stand up, I ask, "What are you doing here? Are you trying to give me a heart attack? Aren't you supposed to be at work?"

"Nope. I was doing a court-appointed and my client

had to have an appendectomy," he answers with a somewhat smug grin. "The judge rescheduled the whole song-and-dance for this time next month."

"So what are you going to do, Mr.-I-live-by-my-calendar? Do you even know what to do with free time?" I tease.

Mark looks pensive for a moment. "I'm not sure I know the answer. I can't remember having any free time in the last decade and a half. First it was college and law school, then Ketki. I've been working like crazy to keep Hunters Crossing up and running. Huh … I guess I haven't slowed down enough to process how much effort it really takes to keep everything going. I took a little time to go to Paris to retrieve Callum's body, but that wasn't a vacation by any stretch of the imagination."

I grimace. "No, I imagine not. My brother has been gone for a decade and a half and I'm still not over it. I can't imagine losing him under the circumstances you did. How are your parents doing?"

"Funny you should ask about my parents, because my mom would like to meet you," Mark answers. "In fact, my mom has summoned us to the house. Apparently, my cousin is participating in his first pow-wow in a while and my mom would like us to be there."

I gasp as I gesture over my body which is barely covered by my robe. "Mark, I am in no shape to meet your mom. I'm in no shape to meet *anybody's* mom, but *especially* not *your* mom." I respond self-consciously, "Have you looked at me recently?"

Mark gathers me gently against him being careful not to touch any of my sore areas. He thoroughly kisses me. "Yes, I see you every day and you grow more beautiful with each passing day."

I shake my head as we sit stuck in traffic. "I still can't believe you talked me into coming. What about the fact that I'm not supposed to be around a ton of people?"

"*Immokalee*, I've been protecting you for months now. I've already given my mom a heads up. She doesn't want anything to happen to you either. I don't think you quite understand what a huge deal it is that my mom has extended an invitation to you."

"I am a little confused. Your mom doesn't know me from Adam and the parts she does know probably seem like bad news. I'm not even sure why she wants to meet me."

"I can answer your question in a single word. Ketki. Shelby, you are amazingly good to my daughter," Mark replies emphatically.

"Mark, how would your mom even know? Who wouldn't be amazingly good to your daughter?" After a moment I add, "Oh, never mind." I let my speech trail off. "Still, how would your mom know about me?"

"Remember how you once described Ketki as more tenacious than a tabloid reporter?" he responds. "Ketki and my mom are active friends on Facebook. Ketki sings your praises often."

"How incredibly generous of Ketki. I adore your daughter."

"I don't think you quite understand what a huge favor Ketki did for you. In our culture, a mother's decision is everything. Without my mother's invitation, you would not have been welcomed into her home."

I nervously fiddle with the bandage under my bra. It's the one area that I can't seem to get healed up. Well, I have two areas but the one on my back I can't see, so unless it starts itching or the searing pain strikes, it doesn't come as readily to my mind as this one under my breast. Finally, I take a deep breath and decide there is no way to delicately address the situation, so I decided to tackle it straight on.

"I respect your mom's right to do that. But it's one thing to bring you and Ketki into all of this, it's a whole other thing to bring your entire family along for the ride. You know I'm not completely out of the woods yet. What if meeting them is a mistake?" I chew on my lip. "You know they'll think you're crazy for dating someone who has cancer? Come to think of it, I think you're a little crazy for dating me —" I confess.

Mark shakes his head violently as he protests, "Shelby, skin cancer is something you have, it isn't who you are. You were a person before you found out about the skin cancer, and you'll still be a whole person after you beat this thing."

Mark's words leave me speechless. It's such a simple little statement yet so profound. It's the reason he can accept me as I am — so freely without reservation. I wish I could turn my brain off and accept it for the beautiful gift it is. Somehow I just can't. The analytical part of me has to push it a little further. "Mark, there is a chance I might not make it, what then?"

The sound Mark makes is low and guttural as he sighs and moans at the same time. Finally, he pulls the car over to the side of the road. He wipes his eyes with his sleeve and then meets my gaze. "Honestly, those thoughts torment my dreams, but love is more than skin deep and when you love someone, you have to take the hard times too. If it comes to the worst, I will be forever grateful you touched my life, however briefly you are in it."

If I thought I was stunned into speechlessness before, I've got *no words* now. This is the kind of grand declaration of love I had always hoped I would hear. Yet, I envisioned being completely happy and healthy when I heard it. I want to be able to say, "*I love you too.*" Yet, without knowing even if I have a future, I don't know what to do. Cancer sucks.

I freeze in place as I try not to cry out as Mark's mom inadvertently tries to rearrange my spine in the process of giving me a hug. I try to cover my expression, but Mark catches my grimace.

"Easy, Mom! Shelby is a little sore, remember?" Mark cautions as he carefully untangles me from his mother's arms.

"Oh, that's right. I remember now. Ketki told me all about it. Although, your yoga is so beautiful I forget how sore you must be," she comments as she looks me over.

I suck in a breath. "My yoga? How did you see my yoga?"

"That granddaughter of mine is so clever, she wears a camera on her head and shows me all sorts of things in life," she explains proudly.

"She's also amazingly sneaky. She didn't tell me she was actually filming. She told me she was merely getting used to wearing it," I mutter under my breath.

"Is Ketki here yet?" Mark asks looking around.

Mark's mother playfully pushes him in the stomach as she remarks, "I think you've been working too hard. Don't you remember the whole reason your daughter is riding with your sister today is because she picked Ketki and her kids up from school? They'll be up later."

Mark snickers. "I figured with Leoti's tendency to have a lead foot, she might actually beat us here."

"Oh, stop picking on your little sister. You know she was only trying to catch the eye of that handsome law man who was giving her tickets."

"Uh-huh. I could never figure out why you always believe everything she tells you. I don't know why no one realizes that I'm actually the good kid."

"If you're the good kid, why haven't you bothered to introduce me?" she challenges.

Mark blushes. "This is Shelby. Shelby, these are my parents. This is my beautiful mother, Hialeah and my father, Adahy."

I try to remember all the lessons my foster mom taught me in her little *Miss Manners* boot camp as I straighten my spine and try not to mumble, "It's nice to meet you." It's hard not to squirm under the scrutiny as Mr. Littleson examines me from head to toe.

He turns to Mark. "It's not like you to bring someone home — especially an outsider. It is clear this one comes with much pain and suffering. Why don't you bring her to the powwow tonight to see Waholi? It would seem Western medicine may not hold all the answers for her. Perhaps it is time for her to consult a *didanawisgi*."

A look of frustration crosses Mark's face. "Dad, I appreciate the suggestion, but Shelby and I haven't even had a chance to talk much about the ways of the

Cherokee. I have no idea whether she even wants to entertain the thought of consulting a medicine man, much less at a public event like a powwow. Can't we just have one night of enjoying ourselves as a family before we have to deal with her cancer?"

Mark's mother has tears in her eyes as she interrupts the conversation, "Oh, nothing much has changed since you were a little boy. You were always my child who was filled with optimism and hope. You must remember … simply pretending the problem does not exist does not make it go away."

Whatever else happens on this trip, I know that I'll have no trouble bonding with Mark's mother. She and I both identified the key weakness with Mark's strategy with my disease. You cannot wish, cajole or bully cancer away. Even so, I am not above trying new — or at least new to me — approaches. Chemotherapy is kicking my butt and maybe ancient and traditional is the way to go.

I smile at Mr. Littleson. "Fate has brought Mark and I far in this relationship. Who am I to doubt it now?"

Chapter Eighteen

Mark

My dad has brown paper spread out over the top of the kitchen table and he's showing Ketki how to properly reassemble a vintage 35 mm camera. Sadly, after forty years in the business, this is a dying art. Everything is digital these days. Shelby is deep in the mix with them, chatting a million miles an hour about f-stops, apertures, filters and depth of field.

I walk up behind Shelby and kiss her on the back of the neck. "If I would've known how easy it was to win your heart, I would've used my inside connections to get you a tricked out new camera."

She squirms away from me as she giggles. "You are a silly, silly man. You're also not very observant if you think a new camera is the one that would make my heart go pitter-patter. It's the old stuff which makes me the happiest. I used to have a camera like the one your dad is tearing down for Ketki right now. Savannah and I found it in a garbage dumpster with a bunch of other broken camera equipment behind a university. Savannah wanted the fancy one with the buttons and bells and whistles, but I wanted the one the news reporters in National Geographic used."

"Somebody just threw away a camera?" Ketki asks, incredulous.

Shelby laughs, reminding me why I call her *Immokalee*. Her laughter is like water in a tumbling creek in the springtime — light, tumbling and speckled with sunshine.

"No, not even almost. There were just camera parts around. I was pretty good at figuring out puzzles so I took a stab at putting it back together. Unfortunately, it didn't work. I was profoundly disappointed because I'd worked so incredibly hard to clean everything up and straighten up crooked parts. One day, we traveled to a new town in search of help for Owen. At one of the homeless shelters, I met up with a veteran who served as a war correspondent. He was fascinated with my camera. He'd worked in the field for so long he seemed to have about a dozen different fixes for every problem. It took about a week and a half, but soon we scavenged together enough parts to make my camera operable. Harvey 'The Ghost' McCade did his best to turn me into a top-notch photojournalist at the age of eleven — and he was off to a pretty good start. Unfortunately, our stint in the town lasted less than a couple months."

"Why didn't you grow up to be a reporter like Lisa Ling?" Ketki asks, riveted by the story.

"Oh, that's a good question. Lisa Ling *is* really cool. She gets to go to all sorts of neat places. I guess I hadn't been at it long enough for the bug to truly bite. We didn't even have the chemicals to develop the pictures. I had to imagine what they'd look like. When my parents decided to leave, I elected to give my camera to The Ghost because he loved it so much."

"It sucks that you had to give up your camera," Ketki remarks.

"Yeah, I was sad — but I was more upset that I had to leave Harvey. He was like a grandpa."

"You poor thing — having to give up your whole family like that — aren't you lonely?" my mom asks and Shelby breaks into a teary smile.

Right now, if it wouldn't be hugely conspicuous, I would love to give my mom a gigantic bearhug. She just gave me the best opening ever. It's funny. My mother does not know that my phone is completely going berserk with text messages — but she has inadvertently given me a hand. We apparently have ourselves a little situation — one I didn't anticipate. Usually, I'm pretty good at heading these things off, but this one blindsided me.

Shelby wipes the machine lubricant off of her fingers and sits back in her chair. She glances up at my mom who is currently covered in flour. "It's a little strange — for years, I never gave it as much thought as I have been recently." Shelby shifts her gaze meaningfully at Ketki as she continues, "I've recently made new friends and they've reminded me what I've been missing without my family. In some ways, that makes it a little harder, I guess."

"It's like having you in *my* life," adds Ketki. "I never wondered about my mom much before, but now I do. It's weird."

This whole conversation and the vibrating phone in my pocket are stark reminders as to why I need to get this whole situation resolved as quickly as humanly possible. Yet, it seems one leg of the journey is well under way, whether I want it to be or not.

"Ketki, for the love of all the things we hold near and dear, please stop whining!" I snap as my head pounds in time with the tires going across the pavement on the freeway. "The noise from these cat-eyes is enough to drive me insane," I complain, as I rub the bridge of my nose and try to focus on the road.

"Cat eyes? I always thought they were called rumble sticks," Shelby remarks absently.

Ketki's expression grows even more dark as she interjects, "Don't you guys know anything? Those are called Bott's Dots — you know, after the guy who invented them?"

Shelby shrugs. "What do you know? I learn something new every day —"

Unfortunately, Ketki is her usual tenacious self and refuses to be distracted by the noisy road or anything else as she continues to argue, "Dad, we hardly ever get to go to Grandma and Grandpa's and you still didn't say why we had to leave early. You can't even use the excuse that you have a trial first thing in the morning because you don't. Your client had surgery," she asserts stubbornly. "Shelby and I were having fun. Why do you always kill the fun?"

"Enough!" I roar. "Ki, I know what I'm doing, okay?"

"Geez, Mark, no need to bite her head off," reprimands Shelby. "She simply asked you a question."

"Well, she's asked me the same question four dozen times," I declare defensively.

"Your point?" Shelby responds with a raised

eyebrow. "That's kind of a Ketki thing and honestly, you have been extremely reticent about all of this. You aren't answering anyone's questions. I mean, it's not uncommon for you to be rather attached to your phone, but you've raised it to a whole new level this weekend. I'm beginning to wonder if I should be concerned. You're checking the thing every two-seconds. I thought you didn't have any trials going on right now."

"I don't. I just have a lot on my mind."

"I know a lot of that's about me," Shelby offers, "but, I still think you might want to send your mom flowers or something. Her feelings seem a little hurt."

"You're right. As you pointed out before, I have a tendency to barrel my way through things. I hope you understand — I always have the best intentions."

"I've been hanging around you long enough — I've figured that out by now," she admits with a snort of laughter.

"In that case, I'd like to preemptively ask for forgiveness in advance."

Shelby vehemently shakes her head. "No way. I may be a brand-new, baby teacher, but even I know better than to give a blank permission slip." She giggles and winks at Ketki. "Nice try, though. I'll give you an A for effort."

"I hope you still feel that way when the dust has settled," I joke, hiding a very difficult truth in plain sight.

The mental argument I've been having with myself is so loud I'm shocked Shelby can't overhear my thoughts. Maybe I should do something to prepare her for what she's about to face, but I have no idea how to do that on the three-hour drive home in front of Ketki. My daughter is already having a colossal meltdown because of this complication and I don't want to escalate things anymore. The time for recrimination and second-guessing is over and it is time to face the music.

"Dad, why is there a car with Georgia plates in our driveway? We don't know anybody from Georgia," Ketki asks, craning her neck to get a better look.

"Were you expecting Tristan? I see his car too," Shelby adds.

"It looks like we may have company," I comment neutrally. As soon as the words escape my mouth, I want to kick myself. Shelby deserves more warning than this, but I don't know how to go back and fix what I've done.

I take a deep breath as I look at Shelby and ask, "Shelby, you know, how sometimes it's weird and things happen which you don't expect? Sometimes good things can come out of bad things — I think today might be one of those days. Do you trust me?"

Shelby narrows her gaze at me. "Of course, as much as I trust anyone, I trust you. I love you — how could I not trust you?"

I let go of the breath I'm holding. "Fair enough. I'll take that."

We abruptly hustle out of the car and Ketki cautions Shelby as we make our way up the front walk.

"I think you might be in trouble, because that's the voice my dad uses when he doesn't want to tell my teacher about something embarrassing I did."

Before I have a chance to explain myself, the front door opens and Savannah bursts out in a flurry of color. I watch with alarm as Shelby becomes ghostly white and sways. Suddenly, I'm grateful for Shelby's slight build as Ketki ducks under her arm and provides support. Shelby struggles to take in the scene in front of her and seems to be rendered utterly speechless. Her mouth is opening and closing like a guppy that suddenly escaped his bowl without notice.

Savannah steps forward and attempts to break the ice as she comments, "Wow! I tried many times to envision the grown-up you, but you didn't look like this. Of course, I always figured you would be skinny, because you always had the energy to spare. I didn't expect curves. You were always such a tomboy I guess I never expected you to grow into a woman. You are so beautiful."

A look of confusion crosses Shelby's face as she tries to process Savannah's words. "Let me get this straight — You haven't seen me in sixteen years and you want to talk about my bust size? *Excuse me?* Is this one of those ambush TV shows? This can't be real! I don't even understand where you're coming from. Wait a second … let me take a minute to get this out — where *are* you coming from? Where have you been? Why aren't you part of my life?"

Just when I thought things couldn't get any more tense, Ketki interrupts the conversation.

"Shelby, is this your sister? I thought you didn't know where she was. If you didn't know where your sister is, how did she find our house? That's really scary. Should we call the police?" Ketki stops her barrage of questions for a millisecond to take a breath before continuing, "Never mind, I guess Tristan is kind of like the police and he knows she's here — so I probably shouldn't call the police. Are you happy your sister is here? Is she going to stay with us too?"

Tears brim in Shelby's eyes as she puts her arm around Ketki's waist and hugs her close. "I wish I knew the answers to your questions Ki, but I am completely in the dark. I hope your dad has some good answers for me."

Instead of looking happy, Shelby looks even more broken than before. Reflexively, I step forward and gather Shelby and Ketki into a large group hug. These two are the external representations of my heart beat. I have to find a way to patch it all back together. This is my family. It's just *not* possible that things wouldn't work out now.

CHAPTER NINETEEN

SHELBY

"I WOULD SAY YOU look beautiful, but honestly, Sissy, you are a mess," Savannah remarks as she studies me carefully.

A burst of surprised laughter escapes my lips as I pour her more coffee in the quiet kitchen. I'm not sure where Mark, Ketki and Tristan disappeared to, but they have vacated the premises, leaving me alone to deal with my sister.

"You always were mean," I respond, sticking my tongue out. "In this case, I can't argue with you. I am a mess. Cancer is no walk in the park."

"I don't think toilet paper band-aids will work this time, Shel," Savannah adds sadly.

I shudder as the childhood memory plays in my mind. "I don't know — the way I remember things, that's probably a good thing. There was an awful lot of spit involved with those. I can't imagine my Wound Care Doctor would approve."

Savannah looks a little shell-shocked as she replies, "You're kidding, right? Do your boo-boos actually have their own doctors?"

I nod as I confirm, "They really do. It's a specialized

area of medicine. I have so many different kinds of incisions and open sores on my body because of the different kinds of treatments they've tried to treat my skin cancer that I have to have someone manage my healing process."

She hides a chuckle behind her hand as she admits, "I'm sorry for laughing, but all I can think about is how horrified Mom and Dad would be if they knew how much you go to the doctor now. It would probably give Dad a heart attack."

I roll my shoulder and feign nonchalance. "How are Mom and Dad doing these days?"

Savannah glances at me with a look of total shock. "You don't know?"

"Know what?" I ask, trepidation filling my voice.

"I never saw them after that nightmarish day."

As I try to process this, she goes on.

"I was carted off to a weird halfway house. Technically, I was still a juvenile, but I was a couple weeks away from turning eighteen, so the court didn't know what to do with me. I tried desperately hard to keep us together — but no one wanted to listen. I didn't have any job skills and no education to speak of because I never even finished fourth grade. There wasn't a sane adult on the planet who would believe me when I told them I had the skills and the fortitude to take care of you at eighteen. The last time I saw you, you were sitting in the back of a police car and there was nothing I could do to stop them from taking you away. My little brother was dead. You were gone. I was left alone in the world."

Just like that, sixteen years of pain, hurt, suspicion and anger fell away from me like a snake shedding an old skin. I pull Savannah up to a standing position and gather her into a hug. I grimace when she touches the most painful spot on my back. Yet, as we hug, she couldn't know Dr. Charleston has taken layers and layers of muscle and skin away leaving me with nerve damage under my shoulder blade which causes me terrible burning pain. It's as if someone holds a burning ember to my back at all times.

I pull away and quietly try to compose myself as I sit down at the table and clutch my cup of coffee. Finally I whisper in a hoarse voice, "I thought you wanted me dead like Owen. I knew he was your favorite and once he was gone. I was sure you didn't want me."

Savannah's eyes widen with shock. "Why in the world would you think that?"

"You know those disposable phones we bought with the money we earned from cleaning Old Man Jenkins store? I've kept it loaded with minutes for sixteen years just in case you called?"

"Da-y-um, I'm sorry I let you down. I always wanted you. I wanted Mom and Dad too, but they vanished like a fog on a hot summer morning. They were gone before the police car was even out of the driveway."

"Wow, it's amazing how one conversation can change everything you thought you knew about your life. Eventually, I ended up with a foster mom. What happened to you?"

Savannah flinches. "It's too long a day for me to have that conversation, but things turned out in the end. I have a cute little shop in Georgia where I help people make arts and crafts, called Paint Your Art Out."

"Like one of those places where couples paint

pictures or make pottery like in the movie *Ghost?*" I ask, unable to hide the excitement in my voice.

A fancy alarm starts to go off on the coffee machine. Savannah and I look at each other with an expression of annoyance, but shrug as we ignore it.

"I can see you're still a terrible, incurable romantic," my sister observes dryly.

"Aren't you?" I retort. "I wasn't alone when we were writing those stories in our tent."

Savannah shakes her head sadly as she replies, "No, I think real life has pretty much beaten any romance right out of me."

"That's sad — you were the person who taught me about princesses, princes and the importance of believing in magic."

Savannah sighs as she examines me, "I don't want to be a downer here, but it seems to me you need a little more than magic here, Sissy. I'm scared for you, really scared."

"I'm frightened too. But —"

The low-key beeping becomes more insistent. "Is that your phone?" Savannah asks, sounding perturbed.

"No, that's not my phone," I answer reflexively as I look around the kitchen. "Oh no," I groan as I remember, "Mark recently got a new phone. I forgot about his new ring tones. He must've left it by the coffee machine before he and Tristan took off with Ketki."

I walk over to the coffee maker and pick up Mark's phone. When I recognize the name on the messenger app, I can't disguise my gasp of dismay.

"Something wrong?" Savannah asks as she sees my

expression.

"I don't know yet," I answer candidly. "There just seem to be about a hundred and five thousand messages from Mark's ex-wife."

Savannah sucks in a dramatic breath as she responds, "Oh, that's never good." She walks up and leans over my shoulder as I'm looking at Mark's phone. "Is she actually that pretty or is it clip art?"

I shake my head as I declare, "No, that's not clip art. She really is that pretty. She is wicked smart too. She's everything I'm not. Tayanita is tall and graceful — almost regal. Her hair is long and shiny and almost down to her butt. You know the kind I mean; she could star in a shampoo commercial."

"Is she an ugly witch inside? Please tell me she's a witch," Savannah replies, fluffing her curly hair. "Some people get all the best genes."

As I reach up to pat my head, a large clump of my hair falls out in my hand. Tearfully, I show it to Savannah as I morbidly quip, "Be careful what you complain about, it could be worse."

Mark's phone beeps again. Savannah looks at me and whispers, "What are you going to do?"

After a brief second of indecisiveness I pick up Mark's phone and answer it, "Mark's phone. This is Shelby."

After listening for a couple of minutes, I answer, "I'm not sure where he is exactly. It sounds like the two of you need to talk."

I pause and listen to her.

It's all I can do not to throw the phone down and just

go running to someplace quiet. This phone call is my nightmare come to life. I never wanted this for anybody.

Finally, I take a deep breath and straighten my spine. "You know what? You and I need to talk. Are you free tomorrow for lunch? Great, I'll see you tomorrow at twelve thirty."

"What happened?" Savannah asks anxiously when I hang up the phone.

"Well, I think I just signed up for an old-fashioned duel over my guy, I hope I come out the victor," I confess, my voice shaking more than I would like.

I had forgotten all the perks of having a sister. I feel and look like a million dollars today. Okay, maybe I don't feel like a million dollars because I spent half the night puking my guts up and there was another pile of hair on my pillow this morning, but Savannah did an amazing job with a random scarf I left in Mark's car. I look put together and fashionable. Two things which rarely ever apply to me — usually I'm just content to look like a leftover flower child from the 70s. Yet, today I am grateful for the additional armor as I sit drinking iced tea waiting for Tayanita.

She is wearing bright orange scrubs as she comes flying through the restaurant. "Shelby, you look much better than the last time I saw you. I'm sorry. This will have to be a quick lunch. The doc I'm working for today wants to work his surgeries close together. Is there something wrong with Ketki? Is that why we're here today?"

Tayanita's question throws me off a little. I wasn't

expecting that. I came here to talk about Mark and I wasn't expecting Ketki's name to be thrown in the middle of it so quickly. I decide to be truthful as I reply, "I'm not sure why we're here, honestly."

"I'm not sure what you expect me to say. You asked me to be here," Tayanita counters.

"I know — and I'm trying to explain without sounding like some psychotic, clingy girlfriend. Please bear with me here. I've had a long night."

"Understandable, you have skin cancer — but what does that have to do with me?" she replies.

"You have to understand that I never expected to have Mark in my life and I certainly never expected to fall in love with him — especially in the middle of a battle for my life. Who is crazy enough to fall in love while they're dying?"

Tayanita just nods her head slightly as she sagely responds, "If you think about it, we all do. We are all dying from the moment we are born. If we are lucky enough to find love, we all do it as we are dying."

"You're not upset?" I ask, thrown off by her easy acceptance of my words.

"Upset that you have cancer? Of course I am. It's hard on Ketki and Mark to watch you suffer. I don't like to see them in pain. I still love them very much."

"*See!*" I exclaim as if I've suddenly found the secret to life. "That right there is why we're here today. We both love the same man and that's not okay with me. At first, when you came back into Mark's life, I thought I could just gracefully step aside and let you all reunite as a family. But I realized I can't do that because Mark *is* my happy. I am not willing to give up my shot at happy. My whole life,

I've let other people decide what happy is for me and I'm *done*. Even though I have cancer — do you understand that?"

Tayanita is still sitting there, all quiet, regal and composed and it pisses me off, so I continue, "*I have cancer!* And I am still happier with Mark than I've ever been in my whole life. I will not step aside for you or anyone else. I love Mark and I love your daughter. Ketki is phenomenal. She makes me smile every day. She makes me think about the world in a different way and she makes me want to fight a million battles just to make the world a fairer place for her. People may think I should step aside and let you all be a family, but you had your shot and you let that opportunity go. Please let me have my happy with Mark."

"Do you think I want Mark back?" Tayanita asks with a confused expression and her mouth agape.

"Well … yes …" I stammer. "Why else would you light up Mark's phone? You don't talk to the man for years and now you can't stop calling him. I only know of one explanation for that. When I look like me and you look like you, the odds are not in my favor —"

Tayanita moves her heavy curtain of hair out of her face with a heavy sigh.

"Obviously it's time for us to have a woman-to-woman talk about your man. Notice I called him *your* man. Once upon a time, he was my man. I really wish I could have been in love with Mark. He is one of the finest men I've ever known. But I never was in love with Mark. Do I love him? Yes, absolutely — I will always love him. He's the father of my daughter."

I openly cringe at her statements, but she holds her

hand up as she continues speaking.

"I have never loved him like a woman should love a man. God knows we tried, we really did. We tried to do all the right things as a couple. We wanted to make our families so happy. We wanted to be the perfect couple. Even though I never really wanted to have kids after having to raise all of my siblings, I was really happy to be pregnant with Ketki because Mark was thrilled. Yet, having Ketki didn't really make us any more of a couple or a family. It wasn't fair to Ketki, I wanted her to be the glue that pulled us together, and when that didn't turn out to be, it made my depression even worse."

"Why not take Ketki with you?" I ask the question that's been burning a hole in my brain since I first heard the story.

"So, this is the hard part to admit even to myself — but it's the truth. Mark is a hundred times the parent I could ever be. I don't have it in me. Maybe I used it all up as a kid with my siblings, I don't know. I never bonded with Ketki, she was like some strange alien doll. Other people would tell me how adorable and cute she was and how blessed I was to have her in my life and all I could think about was how much she hated me."

"That must've been absolutely terrifying and awful," I concede. "Ketki would like a chance to know you, are you aware?"

A dark, thunderous expression crosses Tayanita's face so reminiscent of Ketki's that it would be amusing if the topic was not so serious. "Yes, I am 'aware'. Why the heck do you think I'm totally freaking out? That's why I've been calling Mark. I can't decide whether it's a good idea or a terrible one. I mean, I've been out of her life for so long. Maybe I should just stay out of her life?"

"I don't think that's a good plan —" I start to argue.

"I know, I know — Mark told me about the whole suicide thing. So, I know I need to get over my fears and just face her. How scary can she be? She's only nine. I can't believe she's going to be ten. Where did the time go? My baby will be ten. I missed it all —" Tayanita laments, as a tear rolls down her face.

That's when it all becomes clear to me. All of this is about fear. My lunch with Tayanita, her phone calls to Mark, Ketki's beliefs about her mom — it's all about fear. This woman does not want my boyfriend; if she had wanted him — he waited for her four years and she could've had him. My reunion with Savannah has shown me that things aren't always what they seem on the surface. Tayanita and Ketki need to be together — I'm going to help make that happen.

I reach out and grab Tayanita's hands as I vow, "Stick with me, you and I have an epic party to plan. We need to make one little girl and her dad very happy."

Tayanita looks a little stunned as she echoes my words from before, "You're not upset that I'm going to be part of Ketki's life?"

I can't hide my flush. "I wouldn't be human if I wasn't a little jealous that you and Mark share something with Ketki I'll never have. Still, for Ketki's sake, we need to pull together as a team. Welcome to *Team Everybody Loves Ketki.*"

CHAPTER TWENTY

MARK

"Should I be worried?" I tease as I watch Shelby's fingers fly across the laptop. She is hunched over the computer as she sits cross-legged in the bed. "You look like you're plotting to take over the world."

"Very funny! Have you ever tried to plan one of these things? Now I know why I don't do birthdays. This is insane. Trying to work around Tayanita's schedule makes it even harder." Shelby straightens the baseball cap on her head and more hair falls out. She watches it fall down and hit the keyboard. She scowls at the offending hair as she mumbles, "Dammit, I *knew* I should've listened to the people at the support group. Common sense should've told me that no amount of ice cubes on my head would save me from the side effects of chemotherapy. Will you still love me when I look like a deranged golf ball?"

"First of all, you are much too beautiful to look like a golf ball. Second, even if you did look like a golf ball, I like to play golf."

"Ha-ha," Shelby responds as she sneezes violently. Her sneeze dislodges the baseball cap and another flurry of hair.

She looks down at the aftermath and she frowns as angry tears spring to her eyes. "*Oh Gosh,* why didn't I listen to them when I had a chance. I could've gotten a nice cute little cut and this would not have been so traumatizing. I don't want to go to a salon like this."

I close the file I'm working on and walk over to the bed. As I scoop her up and hold her next to my chest, I note with alarm how light she has become. She has never been heavy, but her weight loss is quite noticeable, even though she tries to disguise it with baggy clothes. It's no wonder she's lost so much weight. The chemotherapy has made her obnoxiously nauseous even though she takes a cocktail of medications to prevent it.

I sit back down on the bed with her on my lap as I offer, "I don't know if you're interested but I'm pretty handy with a pair of clippers. I used to cut Callum's hair all the time. He used to keep it short because he liked to travel embedded with the news crews."

"What if my head is all lumpy and bumpy and disgusting? I don't want you to see my ugly mess. This isn't how the fairytale is supposed to go," she whispers as she buries her head in my chest.

"You're right, it's been a little unorthodox. Even so, I can't help but think things are down right idyllic between us despite your cancer." I declare as I capture her lips in a kiss. I break the kiss and look her in eyes. "Shelby, I don't care if you have scars on your face or your breasts or your back. I don't care if your hair reaches your chin or your shoulders — or your knees for that matter. I don't mind if it's curly, straight, brown, black, or blonde. In fact, I couldn't care less if you have any hair at all. I didn't fall in love with your hair or your skin. Love is more than skin deep. You demonstrate it with everything that you do and say."

Shelby shakes her head as if to push my words away. She whispers in a broken voice, "I just want to be beautiful for you."

I wipe away Shelby's tears with the pads of my thumbs as I struggle to verbalize my thoughts. This may be harder than any closing argument I've ever delivered, but far more important.

"*Immokalee*, look at me. Listen carefully. There will never be a time that you are not beautiful to me. You are the definition of beauty. Do you understand? You are beautiful because you are you. It has nothing to do with what you look like and everything to do with who you are."

I have to take a moment to swallow hard and catch my breath before I can continue. "You are beautiful because you see my daughter for the miracle she is. You take the time to understand her sorting system and to answer her endless questions. You respect her talent and encourage her to be proud of who she is. You make her feel strong and empowered. You help my daughter feel beautiful," I explain. "*That's* the kind of beautiful I'm looking for. The rest of it is only skin deep."

"Mark, I have made your life so much more complicated," Shelby argues. "Some days, I bet you wish you'd never even laid eyes on me."

"Hush. If anything, you are a beautiful complication in my life, Shel," I state emphatically. "Ketki and I had slipped into survival mode. I don't even think we realized how lonely and isolated we'd become until you popped into our lives. We were so used to counting on only each other that we forgot what it was like to include other people. Do you know how much it means to me that you always ask how I feel after I've interviewed a new client or lost a close case? You always support me whether I win or lose. It gives me a sense of being grounded. With everything else in my life coming down to winners and losers, profits and losses, ups and downs — it's nice to know you're always here holding steady."

Shelby wrinkles her nose at me and lets out a startled burst of laughter. "Mark, you make me sound like I'm a strange financial institution set to give you advice on stocks and municipal bonds for your retirement instead of your lover. I'm sorry. I know you meant that to be all romantic, but it's just funny."

The woman has a point. For a man who expresses himself in words every day, I'm botching this badly. I feel a blush overtake my body as I respond, "Guilty as charged. For some reason, I can manage to break down the most complicated legal issues and explain them without difficulty, yet I struggle to tell you exactly how much I love you. All I can do is show you the pictures in my mind and hope you understand."

"Mark, I was only teasing —" she protests weakly, still smiling. She sobers as she senses my mood shift.

"No, *Immokalee*, this is important. I want you to hear me out. You need to know you are what holds my little family together and makes it work so well. Technically, Ketki and I were functioning adequately before, but you make us a family. You know how my dad's thing is cameras? Well, my grandfather's thing was watches — most specifically Swiss watches. I used to watch in complete fascination as he would take apart all these intricate gears and put them back layer after layer until each watch ran perfectly. It's as if you are the perfect gear for our family — the one missing thing. You smooth out the hitches and help everything sync perfectly between all of us. You hold us all together."

Shelby's brows furrow and she bites her lip. This is her trademark maneuver when she's trying to solve a puzzle. Finally, she begins to talk, haltingly at first, "When you first started talking, I was a little offended, honestly. You said none of the romantic lines I've been trained to expect from a guy. In fact, on the surface, a few of them seem exactly the opposite. Your words are unorthodox, but as I listened to you I realized the reason you're having a hard time defining our relationship in typical terms is because our relationship is not typical. It explains why I never was a good fit with anyone else; I was meant to fit with you and Ketki."

I plant a symbolic kiss on the top of Shelby's baseball cap before I declare, "I won't argue with that *Immokalee*. Now, will you let me help you with your hair?"

Shelby reaches up and touches her hat as if she forgot her hair was the whole reason we began having this conversation.

Abruptly, she breaks out into a fit of giggles. "I give up. It's not as if you don't *know* I have cancer."

I knew this would be hard, but I didn't think it would be *this* hard. Even opening the grooming kit was hard. *Stupid, freakin' terrorists.* I can handle losing in court. If I lose in court, it generally means the facts of my case were weak or the law wasn't on my side. To lose my baby brother to a bunch of nameless faceless terrorists — I guess they're not really faceless any more, because I've seen their mug shots plastered all over the news — is a whole different kind of losing. It's losing without reason or justification. It will never, *ever* make sense. I can't explain it to my mom and dad and I can't explain it to my sister and my nieces and nephews. More importantly, I can't make sense of the senseless for my daughter, who loved her uncle with unparalleled dedication.

I can hear Callum's teasing voice in my head as I put a new blade on the clipper. During the last haircut I gave Callum before he was killed, he warned me to keep a hunk of his hair in case he ever got famous and we had to prove we were his relatives. Of course, it didn't exactly play out the way he planned, but in the end, investigators ended up confiscating his personal razor blade for DNA to help identify his body.

My hands tremble as the memory slams through my brain. I look up in the mirror and catch Shelby's stricken gaze. "I'm sorry. This is going to cause you pain. I don't want to hurt you," she declares with big tears rolling down her face. "Why does this stupid disease have to hurt everyone I know?"

Her hollow voice haunts my soul. I might have a beef with terrorists half a world away, but Shelby is fighting a battle every single second of every single day right in front of me. I need to get my head in the game.

I paste a smile on my face and run my hand over my own hair as I offer, "Maybe I should shave mine off too — you know, as a show of solidarity with you. What's good for one is good for all and all that jazz—"

Shelby looks positively horrified as she responds,

"Don't you dare! I don't want to be reminded my hair is gone every time I look at you. I love your hair. Don't make that sacrifice for me. It proves nothing. It would just make me sad."

"I guess you're right, I didn't think of it from that perspective. I want you to know — I'd willingly take on this burden for you if I could," I respond as I start to snip off locks of her hair.

Shelby looks at me in the mirror with a watery smile and remarks, "One of the women from my support group had a head full of stick-straight hair before chemo. When it all grew back, she said it was a completely different color and curly. Maybe when mine grows back, it will be straight and gorgeous like Ketki's."

I tilt her head back and kiss her on the forehead as I respond, "You know, I don't care. I will take you however I can get you. You will always be gorgeous to me."

Shelby leans back against my chest with half of her head clipped and the other in complete disarray. Her eyes meet mine in the mirror. "I don't know what it is about you, Mark Littleson, but you make me want to believe in impossible things," she declares as a tear rolls down her cheek.

"Ditto" I whisper softly as I wipe it away with my thumb. I have nothing to add. I could not have said it better myself.

"Un-freakin-believable!" Shelby exclaims as she slams the laptop shut, causing her tea to slosh over the side of the cup.

I look up from the brief I'm outlining. "What's up?"

"I thought Kristi was supposed to be Ketki's friend," Shelby huffs with a scowl toward her computer.

"Last I checked she was," I answer, my focus half on my work.

"Mark, you need to pay attention to this." Shelby declares with disgust, her body vibrating with tension. "That was an email from Kristi's mom declining Ketki's birthday invitation, because it would be bad for her daughter's social reputation."

"*What?* That doesn't sound like Vivian. The girls have played together since they were babies," I protest.

"Well, she wasn't quite that rude, but that's essentially what she said," Shelby clarifies. "Ketki's teacher wasn't any more encouraging. She yammered on about the classroom being a mirage of friendship for Ketki and encouraged me to look elsewhere."

I sigh. "I should've known this would happen. Last year was an unmitigated disaster. I guess I was hoping she was becoming a little more social and making more friends. Ketki tried to warn me it wasn't getting any better; I just wasn't listening. Some days, I feel like the worst parent on the planet."

Shelby shakes her head. "Mark, I am a professional, and even I didn't realize it was quite this bad. Ketki keeps it all under wraps. She makes a few cryptic remarks here and there, but she doesn't share much. It's too bad Ketki can't hang out in-person with all of her buddies from Tristan's beta-testing team. We all have a great time. We did a game SIM last weekend. It was a blast. Ketki is the natural leader of the group there."

"It would take some juggling with school schedules, but why couldn't you? Thanksgiving break is coming up,"

I suggest.

Shelby's mouth drops open. "I don't think you understand. There are about a dozen people in the group from all over the United States. It would be unbelievably expensive. I know you like to make sure Ketki's needs are met, but this would go above and beyond."

I sit forward in my chair as I puzzle through the idea in my head. "It wouldn't necessarily have to be *my* dime, right? Doesn't Tristan have that new software facility opening soon in California?"

"Yes —" Shelby answers cautiously. "That's why we've been testing so extensively. Tristan wants to show the new project on the big screens during the grand opening."

I grin ear to ear as a thought occurs to me. "Problem solved. The perfect birthday party awaits. Do you know what else is in California?"

"Disneyland?" Shelby guesses with a wide smile.

"That's true, but Ketki isn't really a princess kind of girl. She's more of a bookworm —"

I can see the wheels turning in Shelby's mind as she ponders my clue. The second she gets it, her face lights up with delight. "Mark, if you have her party at Universal Studios and take her to Harry Potter Land, you would be elevated to Father of the Millennium."

I pretend to polish my fingernails on the front of my shirt as I say, "Let's do this!"

I decide with finality this has to happen. "Just so you know, if I'm able to pull this one off, it will definitely be a team effort. Any ideas about how to make sure Tristan is in a great mood?"

Shelby rolls her eyes before she rubs her hands together, cracks her knuckles and reopens her computer. "I've heard a rumor that he's quite fond of his mother-in-law's tamales."

Chapter Twenty-One

Shelby

I LAUGH AS ONE of Jessica's macramé beads rolls down the aisle of the plane. "You are dealing with this so much better than I would," I compliment as I stop the bead with my foot.

Jessica's hands never stop moving as she repetitively ties decorative knots. She doesn't even slow down as she answers my question, she merely shrugs. "I can't think of a better way to get married. I take that back — Isaac and Rosa have us beat. You know, Mitch and I can't top Paris. Still, if you want to put all my friends on a big plane and fly them to California, I won't complain —"

"Are you sure you want me to be one of your bridesmaids? Have you looked at me lately? I have no real hair — I only have peach fuzz," I announce as if she can't see what's right in front of her.

"Peshaw, you are magnificent! You look just like Kelly Pickler when she donated all of her hair to charity. Come to think of it, you really *do* look like Kelly Pickler. I'm a little jealous. I'd like to get rid of this mane sometimes."

I roll my eyes as I quip, "Yeah, I used to say that too,

and now look what happened."

Jessica covers her mouth in horror. "Oh man, me and my big mouth. I'm sorry. You'd think I'd learn."

"Don't worry about it. I'm friends with Jade and you wouldn't *believe* what comes out of her mouth —"

"Hey now! I might want to object to your characterization of me," protests Jade as she pops a chocolate covered pretzel in her mouth and plops into the seat next to me.

"Did you or did you not suggest auctioning off sections of my scalp on YouTube for tattoos?" I ask pointedly.

"Oh come on! That was one of my best ideas ever, even Marcus thought it was a good idea!" Jade exclaims.

"My head is not a billboard!" I insist.

Yuki, the service dog Jessica is training tries to nuzzle my hand in an effort to calm me down.

"At the risk of sounding like Gabriel Iglesias, 'would've been funny,'" interjects my sister.

"Right? She could've made some serious bank and had a radically cool statement piece at the same time," Jade agrees. "I don't see the problem. Her hair will grow back."

I throw my hands up in the air in frustration as I growl, "The problem is, I have a cue ball for a head and I'm not about to let you color all over it like it's a jack-o'-lantern."

Ketki taps me on the shoulder before she whispers in my ear in a very loud stage whisper, "I'm not very good at this, but even *I* can tell they're just kidding. Relax a little, it's a party. We're supposed to be having fun."

Mark squeezes my hand. "Are you having a good time?"

"I've said it before, and I'll say it again. Your friends are down-right strange."

Mark slings his arm around my waist as we walk around the deserted parking lot to cool down. "Perhaps, but then again, that might be why we fit in so well — though I'm curious to know why you think so?"

"Admittedly, my upbringing has limited the number of times I've been invited to a bachelorette party, but I have a relatively good idea of what to expect from one of these parties. This wasn't it," I reply.

"What's wrong, Shelby? Were you disappointed that there weren't any strippers? If that's the only problem, I can arrange a private show for you later," Mark teases as he wiggles his eyebrows at me suggestively.

Good thing it's dark and he can't see my blush because his words make me turn bright red. Not that I am opposed to a little private show on principle, but the execution of it is a little trickier. I'm not quite as bold as I'd like to pretend to be. I guess a bit of my quasi-religious upbringing has seeped into these pores after all.

"Maybe another time," I stammer, sidestepping the issue. "In case you haven't noticed, your daughter is with us on this trip. Which brings me back to my point — your friends *are* weird. I've seen plenty of movies and television shows — this is not what happens at bachelorette parties. I don't think it's typical to have boys at the party, let alone to rent out entire trampoline gyms for a horde of teenagers who've never met in person."

Mark laughs out loud. "No, this has Tristan's

fingerprints written all over it. Actually, if you think about it, it's probably more about Marcus. Doesn't Marcus have his little brother from the Big Brother/Big Sister Program here?"

"You mean the one who is starting his freshman year at Stanford? I think Marcus has issues saying goodbye," I joke with a smirk.

"Hey, don't laugh. I sat next to that kid at dinner. He's exceptionally bright. He puts my current associate to shame. Let's just say, I hope he doesn't lose my business card before he finishes college and — knock-on-wood — law school."

"Speaking of bright kids, you didn't tell me Ketki is like an Olympic gymnast. She was jumping rings around everyone else out there, including the adults," I say with pride.

"You know how Ketki feels about feathers and stones?" Mark replies. "She felt the same way about trampolines first."

"Ahh, That explains a lot." Some of Ketki's comments from earlier suddenly make sense in light of this new information. "I'm glad she could handle the extra stims in front of her new friends. She's doing a fabulous job around everything new."

"It was nice of Rosa and Isaac to volunteer to babysit tonight. I hope Isaac is ready to get beat at chess. Ketki pulls no punches. She plays like every game is her last."

"I wouldn't worry about it," I assure him. "I'm sure they can handle whatever comes up. I could see them at dinner and they were off in their own little world. I asked Rogue about it and she said she'd never seen Tristan and

Isaac be that thick as thieves with anybody so quickly. I guess Ketki's eye for detail might actually help them on a case or two. Whatever Isaac can't handle, I'm sure Rosa can."

Mark pulls me into an embrace as he backs up against a brick wall. "So *Immokalee,* we are in California, the land of dreams and fantasies — and without our child for the evening, how would you like to take advantage of that?"

I'm not even sure how to answer that question. Sometimes I wish I could turn the analytical side of my brain off. I'm still a little stuck on the words dreams and fantasies. Do I have fantasies about Mark Littleson? *Oh yes.* I have many. Often. More than I care to admit. Some are unabashedly hot, several are sweet, and a few are far more practical. He has become my favorite fantasy. Actually, he has become my favorite subject for dreaming *period.* Mark Littleson is my dream. My smoking hot, hunky, phenomenally great-smelling dream.

I'm still lost in my somewhat lusty thoughts when Mark clears his throat. "Well?"

I have to focus to drag my attention back to the topic at hand as I answer. I pretend to contemplate the dilemma, but the answer is pretty simple for me. I want to go dancing with all of my new friends. It's only been during the last couple of weeks that I've started to feel human even though my last chemotherapy treatment was weeks ago.

I take the time to straighten the collar on Mark's shirt. He picked it up on his last trip home. One of his mom's friends hand beads the collars in a manner similar to how she works with the regalia used for formal Cherokee ceremonies. The result is simply stunning. He looks rugged and handsome. Mark smirks at me as he watches me devour him with my eyes. He takes a moment to roll-up the sleeves on his shirt.

My mouth goes dry at the sight and I have to struggle to remember what I was going to say. It takes a moment before it all comes back. I stop him from going back into the club and pull him back toward the shadows beside the restaurant as I remark, "This is an unprecedented situation for us. We haven't had a lot of opportunity to spend time together without a child present. It's a good thing we've got lots to celebrate today. I didn't even get a chance to tell you but Dr. Charleston's office called. They were so impressed with the last round of scans. They called to let me know that the suspicious spots in my lymph nodes are looking rather unremarkable. As Dr. Charleston said, they are markedly better."

Mark smiles a tight smile but even in the dim light of the entryway, I can tell it's his fake polite smile. It doesn't take a rocket scientist to figure out what the problem is.

I pull his face in and plant a soft kiss on his lips as I say, "Don't worry, I had them check three times to make sure that the results were actually from me. It's real."

"For real? Black and white, verifiably real?" Mark questions.

I nod. "For real, backed up by pictures and blood work."

Mark leans his forehead against mine as he says, "I've never been so glad to hear good news in my whole life. Although, it's too bad we're not at Ink'd — it would've been so fine to ring the bell loud and clear."

I laugh lightly as I agree, "I'm sure they'll allow us to

ring it retroactively. We seem to have an 'in' with a few members of the management. Do you have your dancing shoes on? I bet they are waiting for us. I didn't spend the last few months worshiping at the feet of the porcelain God without planning to dance in the face of cancer in the end. So, for lack of a better term — let's party!"

CHAPTER TWENTY-TWO

MARK

IT'S CRAZY WHEN YOU discover the things you don't even realize you're doing until you stop doing them. In my case, I've been holding my breath for months on end. I can't tell you how much relief I felt when Shelby told me her scan showed so much improvement. Of course, there's always a chance for a setback or a relapse, yet it's as if we've finally been given breathing room.

Breathing room. This trip has been all about breathing room. The freedom to be ourselves. Okay, I know every single parent feels this way to a certain extent, but because of the unique situation with Ketki, I often feel especially stuck. I know I can ask my sister to watch her, but Leoti has her own children and Ketki can be a handful. Since I sometimes have to be away for work, guilt always seems to get the best of me if I want to leave Ketki just so I can have a social life.

I've been so busy providing for Shelby that I failed to notice my own support system has become much larger as well. Although we had planned for Ketki to stay in our suite, she elected to stay with Isaac and Rosa. This is a welcome development since Ketki was the one who initiated the extended contact. After Mama Rosa offered to teach her how to do embroidery, my daughter grabbed her suitcase and disappeared so quickly my head almost spun. As I watched her leave with little fanfare or drama, I realized I was having a completely typical, average moment with my soon-to-be ten-year-old daughter and the simple beauty of that almost took my breath away.

I think Shelby understood what I was feeling because our lovemaking last night was more connected than it's ever been. It was as if our lips and fingertips were connected to our hearts and souls. We didn't have to speak to communicate. It was the most in tune I've ever been with anyone. Maybe it's because I finally believe Shelby will survive skin cancer. I finally have the breathing room to show her how much I truly feel.

Instinctively, I pull Shelby closer. Her cheek slides across my chest and her eyes pop open. She squints at the alarm clock before complaining, "I still could've slept for another eleven minutes. Do you know how late it was last night when we got to bed? We are taking a bunch of teenagers to a theme-park today. How crazy are we? We totally should have planned this better."

"Uh-huh," I answer in a low tone as I remember how the night ended. "Seems like someone I know wanted to dance until dawn."

"Nobody warned me not to challenge Jade to a dance-off. That was one of the dumbest ideas I've had in forever. I should have strategized a little better."

"Mmm-hmm," I mumble, as I rub a knot out of her calf.

"Speaking of strategies, what time is Tayanita coming?" Shelby asks as she stretches and yawns.

"Her flight doesn't get in until eight-thirty. Tristan

said he was planning to send one of his body men to go get her."

Shelby's eyes sparkle with delight. "Oh, how fun!"

Feeling lost, I ask, "What are you talking about?"

Shelby rolls her eyes and lobs her pillow at me as she inquires with exasperation, "Haven't you watched any chick-flicks made in — I don't know — the last sixty years?"

"Of course I have, I have a sister," I answer, still missing the point.

She looks at me like I'm one of her students who can't quite grasp the art of finger-painting. "Well, the bodyguard always falls in love with his beautiful charge and as much as it pains me to admit this, your wife is drop dead gorgeous."

"Shelby, Tayanita is very pretty, but she will never be as beautiful as you. You're missing a key word in that sentence. Tayanita is my *ex-wife*. We've been divorced for years. She's only coming to this to support Ketki — you *know* that. You had to talk her into coming."

"I know. It's just hard sometimes, especially when I look like this," Shelby confesses as she runs her hand across her head. Her hair has grown back, but it's still quite short and baby-fine.

I narrow my gaze. "Shel, do you really think I care?"

Shelby shakes her head "I know you. don't, but some days I do."

"Can you try to make this day a day you don't care?" I suggest carefully. "Everybody and their dog will have a baseball cap on today, no one will even notice. Everyone is here to see Harry Potter anyway. I'm surprised Ketki isn't here banging down the door wondering what's taking us so long."

Shelby digs through her suitcase and pulls out some clothes. "You're right. Nobody cares what I look like — except maybe you. You like to look at me naked," she teases as she chuckles with a low husky laugh which makes me second-guess all of my good intentions. She glares over at the clock. "I guess showering for two is off the table for now," she casually remarks with a sexy wink.

She laughs out loud when I groan audibly.

"There is good news. It seems like sleepovers at Padre Pop and Mama Rosa's might materialize and we could schedule a rain check," Shelby teases as she waltzes toward the bathroom with her towel and her clothes draped over her arm.

"Remind me to send Mama Rosa a huge bouquet of flowers and Isaac a handwritten thank you note," I grumble, as I watch her shapely backside disappear.

"Rosa likes those little tiles with inspirational sayings for her garden," Shelby suggests, barely hiding her bubble of laughter.

"I'll keep that in mind," I answer slowly as I replay the whole conversation in my head, curious about what I'd overlooked.

"Mark, think about it. Issac and Rosa are the ideal babysitters." Shelby comes back to the bed and kisses me thoroughly before she remarks, "I just thought I'd point it out … considering Christmas break is coming right up and I've never been to Hawaii. I think I love Hawaii. I hear that they've got all sorts of great hotels with magnificent showers for two," she teases.

I grin ear to ear. "Do you think Rosa needs an

underground watering system?"

Shelby winks at me again. "I don't know. I'll ask — we could use a really *long* vacation."

I probably could've saved myself a bunch of sleepless nights if I'd really paid attention to Tristan and Isaac's background. Intellectually, I knew they had military connections and training. I know Tristan is highly entrenched in the law enforcement community and has the respect of politicians and front-line folks alike. I know less about Isaac Roguen, but I know he worked for some agency which had alphabet soup as a name. Still, it's hard for me to reconcile the video game playing, sangria-drinking, salsa-dancing fun people I know with the straight-laced, serious professionals I see in front of me today.

Even though I'm looking forward to introducing Ketki to all of her favorite things at Universal Studios in California, I'm nervous about her safety on this trip. She can get focused on small seemingly meaningless minutia and the world around her fades. She forgets to watch out for her own well-being. It's overwhelmingly scary. Ketki has been known to literally wander into traffic, even at ten years old. Had I known Tristan and Isaac would run this like a fine-tuned military operation, I might not have been quite so worried.

The participants all have special Identity Bank shirts on, which indicate which team they're playing for. There seem to be five people on each team. I swallow a chuckle. My daughter's team colors appear to be hot pink. I bet that went over well — not. The teams seem balanced between children and adults, with two adults per team.

I hear Shelby suck in a breath beside me as she hisses, "Do you see what I see?" She points her finger toward the group. "What do you think this means? Did you *know* about this?"

"*Heck no*, I didn't know," I snap. I try not to blow my stack as I see my ex-wife wearing a green shirt, similar to the one my daughter is wearing. I take a few breaths to try to calm myself down before I speak to anyone. The last thing I want to do is ruin my daughter's birthday party. I set off to find someone in charge who can explain this whole debacle.

Finally, I locate Marcus sitting on top of a cooler with a clipboard. Ironically, he is wearing a polo shirt which says, *Need info? Ask me!*

I gulp in another deep breath before I blurt, "You know anything about the game?"

Marcus grins. "I should hope so by now. It seems like I've been working on it forever with Super-Secret-Spy-Guy."

"Marcus, This is *serious* stuff," I warn in a lethal tone.

He immediately stands up and walks me over to the formal command station which looks like a big horse trailer. It's my turn to be shocked as I ask, "Didn't we just fly across the country? How does he have all this in place? I thought we were simply having a birthday party for Ketki."

"I'm not even shocked any more, I don't bother to ask. It's Tristan Macklin. He just does what he does. It's always impressive. So, you had a question?" Marcus prompts.

"Do you know anything about the players?" I ask.

"All them are completely checked out before they're

allowed into the software testing program, why?"

I openly sneer as I challenge, "You missed one, Sherlock."

"WTF?" Marcus asks with alarm.

"See that tall one, with the braid down her back? She has no business being here," I declare, pointing at Tayanita.

Marcus follows my finger with his gaze and looks back at me with surprise as he says, "Are you talking about Scrubs? Why would you ask about her? She's been with our organization for over five years. She's been working with Tristan to develop software to help families use social media to connect to lonely family members with health concerns."

"So, you are telling me she didn't weasel her way in to play the game with my daughter?" I demand impatiently.

"No, of course not. Scrubs has been on the Alpha team since the beginning. She's been a huge gamer from the start. I think it is one of the ways she relaxes from her day job. She's one of our most talented players," Marcus answers. "Maybe you should try it, you seem a little stressed out."

"Does she know she's playing with kids? She doesn't even like kids," I reveal.

"Dude, that's harsh!" Marcus reprimands. "But — no this is the first time most of these people have met. Most of us have identities separate from our real selves, and we don't really discuss our true age or identity online. It's especially true at Identity Bank. Tristan wanted his participants to be judged only on skill, so he had them develop gender and age neutral identities."

"That's smart," I comment.

"Didn't you read all that paperwork Tristan sent over when he signed Ketki up for the program? Our guidelines are outlined in there," Marcus explains with a curious glance. "I still don't understand why you are going ape over Scrubs. If anybody belongs in the software testing program at Identity Bank, it's Scrubs. The only other person I've met who is as much of a natural at all of this is Stones."

"Stones?" I repeat blankly.

Marcus lets out a surprised gust of air as he comments, "Boy, you sure don't listen to Ketki talk about her gaming stuff much, do you? Stones *is* Ketki. Before you ask, your girlfriend is rather kick-butt at this as well. Although she hasn't been on a formal testing team because she's been feeling so lousy, she sometimes helps us out. Her moniker is 'Dream Catcher.'"

I scrub my hand over my face as I admit, "I feel like I'm living in an alternate universe. Do Stones and Scrubs ever play together? Do they know each other? Are they sometimes on the same team?" I pinch the bridge of my nose to cope with my headache.

Marcus shrugs nonchalantly. "I suppose it's possible. The players are involved in round-robin play and play at will. They play whoever is available at any given time. We don't prescribe any certain type of play — it would mess with the game flow. I don't know. That stuff is all beyond me. Tristan studies all of it. I'm mostly a gamer, I never even knew about all this stuff until I met Tristan. Why are you suddenly so curious about this?"

"I'm wigging out, as Ketki would put it, over the possibility that over the past few months, my daughter has been hanging out and playing computer games with my ex-wife," I answer as I pace in front of him.

"Scrubs is Stones' *mom*? The one Ketki thought had committed suicide? Wow!" Marcus exclaims. "This is great!"

"Would you care to tell me on what planet this is great? I don't mean one of your pretend worlds. I mean like the real one I have to live in," I challenge.

"I *do* mean this one, Doofus," Marcus responds with a grin. "If you'd stop panicking over not being in charge of the universe for a moment, you'd see I'm right. This is probably the best of all outcomes."

"*Right*. Whatever you say." I add sarcastically.

"Think about it for a moment. Your ex-wife and her daughter are already friends of sorts. They have something in common and something to talk about. If nothing else, they can talk about the game. That's more than most parents can talk about with their kids. As a special bonus prize, your ex-wife and your current girlfriend both play the game. How often does that happen? They have stuff to talk about too. You're so lucky! I think you should go stock up on lottery tickets or something."

I stop a moment to ponder what Marcus is saying. *It's a lot to hope for but... still if it all works out.*

"Marcus, you're a funny looking dude with all of your tattoos and piercings, but when you're right, you're right," I utter out loud as excitement builds in my stomach.

Marcus performs a little bow as he says, "Thank you, I try. I wonder… what's the best way to break this sort of news?"

"Oh man! I don't know." I exclaim. "They don't have

manuals for this kind of thing."

"Let me ask the Boss-man," Marcus suggests as he talks into a walkie-talkie. When he finishes, he looks up at me and says, "It turns out that the cyber-world has a little less draw in the face of a real life theme park and everyone wants to go explore, so Tristan says everyone is free for the next couple of hours anyway."

This news stops me in my tracks. I guess I was counting on the structure of the game to protect me a little while longer. I have no game plan. My mind is whirling at a thousand miles an hour. The potential for this to go catastrophically wrong is exponentially high. Everyone has so much to lose.

Suddenly, I hear Marcus whistle through his teeth quietly as he mutters, "Look at that — trust the women to figure it out before we do."

Sure enough, as I follow his gaze, I see his wife, Ivy taking family shots of my ex-wife and my daughter with her cell phone. Every once in a while, she includes Shelby in the pictures. From this distance, they all seem to be surviving the encounter.

"Come on, man. It's your daughter's birthday, you can't avoid this. Look at it this way, it must be fate, right?"

"I suppose you could call it that, or you might call it the universe's giant practical joke —" I mumble as I cautiously make my way toward my family.

Ketki sees me from several yards away and starts to call my name. "Dad! Dad! Dad!" She comes and gets me and pulls me toward Tayanita and Shelby.

Marcus salutes me, "Good Luck," as he quietly watches the interaction with Ivy by his side.

Ketki is a little breathless as she informs me, "You'll

never believe what just happened. This is my mom! In California! Weird, huh?"

Before I can even almost explain, she continues her non-stop play-by-play, "So, we were playing the game and I noticed she looks like me. Like, you know, we don't see so many people from Cherokee Nation. I recognized her user name from the game because I sometimes watch the TV show and I thought her alias was funny. We played together before — because I talked to her about being a nurse in RL. She's really good at the game; almost as good as me."

"Ketki, take a breath," I caution.

My daughter takes a dramatic deep breath in and blows it out before she continues speaking, "So, I see this Cherokee who looks like me. I decide to be brave and introduce myself. You know I don't like crowds, but I figure she's a gamer, so I go for it because Tristan knows her and she must be okay. Then the weirdest thing *ever* happens, I told her my name and she turned almost as white as Shelby. I thought she was going to fall down on the ground — you know how Shelby felt after her operations when she could barely stand up? That's kinda how Mom looked. I was very confused. I was polite and everything when I said hello, so I didn't know what was going on."

Shelby places a protective arm around Ketki's shoulder as she replies, "Ketki, you didn't do anything wrong, honey — neither did Tayanita. I think she was surprised to find out that you had grown into such a lovely young lady."

Tayanita steps forward and kneels beside Ketki. "I'm sorry I scared you. I was planning to surprise you for your birthday, but it turns out you're the one who surprised me. I was nervous about coming here, because the last time I saw you, you weren't much older than a baby. I figured you wouldn't even remember anything about me and I was afraid you might not even want to know me because of what happened. I never expected we would already know each other — even if it's only through the Internet. I didn't expect that you and I would have so much in common. I guess I always thought you would be just like your dad since I wasn't in your life."

Ketki awkwardly pats Tayanita on the head, but there's a stubborn tilt to her chin as she asks, "Why weren't you here?"

Tayanita takes a deep shuddering breath. "I don't know if I can explain it all to you. After you were born, the chemicals in my brain went a little crazy and I got really sad. I couldn't do anything to make myself feel better. To keep you safe, I left you with your dad. I went to school to become a nurse. I needed to figure out why I felt so bad. I finally learned I'd had something called postpartum depression. By that time, I had been gone so long, I was embarrassed that I wasn't a good mom. You and your dad were doing so well together I didn't want to disturb you guys. I always loved you, but I never knew how to make us work as a family," she admits candidly, wiping away her tears.

"Why are you here now?" Ketki asks, astutely.

"I heard you thought I hated you and I wanted to show you it isn't true. I *never* hated you. I just couldn't cope with the depression. I'm sorry if you thought anything else," Tayanita discloses in a shaky voice.

I can tell Ketki is weighing her Mom's words carefully. After a few moments, she looks up at me and asks "Dad, is that depression stuff like the thing we saw on YouTube where the lady drowned her kids in the bathtub?"

I nod curtly as I remember the horrific documentary I caught Ketki watching one night. "Postpartum depression very likely played a role, yes."

Ketki's brows furrow in concentration. After several moments she posits, "It's probably a good thing Mom left for a while. Otherwise I might be dead." Ketki's hands move rhythmically before she closes them into fists and jams them in her pockets. After a minute of awkward silence, she blurts, "I have another question —"

I crack a smile. "Why am I not surprised? You seem to always have another question —"

Ketki wrinkles her nose at me as she recognizes that I'm teasing her. "This is pretty important, Dad. Is it all right if I have more than one mom? I like Tayanita, but I really want Shelby to be my mom too."

I reach out to stroke my daughter's cheek as I respond, "Working on it, Ki. Totally working on it," I assure her. "How about if we tackle one problem at a time? Right now, you've got a birthday party to attend."

Ketki starts bouncing excitedly on the balls of her feet as she announces, "*I know!* It's like the most epic birthday ever. Tristan said it would be fun to make this an annual thing. Did you know that annual means to do it every year? Next year I want Mom to be on my team. Isn't it funny? We're on different teams, Maybe next year, you and Shelby can join my team too — we could be like one huge family team."

To be ten years old again and have everything in life boil down to a few lines of video game code and screen names. *It would be nice if real life could be scripted as easily.*

Come to think of it, real-life isn't so awful for me these days.

CHAPTER TWENTY-THREE

SHELBY

I'M TRYING EXCEPTIONALLY HARD to be a supportive partner, but what I really want to do is laugh. Mark looks like he wants to commit justifiable homicide. I gently take the phone out of his hands and hand him a glass of wine.

As soon as I put the phone on the table, it starts to ring again. "You've got to be kidding me!" he grouses. "What part of 'vacation' did they not understand? I realize I haven't been on very many of them lately, but perhaps the other partners could step up and do their part for a change."

"Hold still or I'll never get this cufflink in," I instruct. "They can't help it if you've been so responsible over the years that they don't know what to do without you," I tease.

"Yeah, I was responsible enough to bring in one of Isaac's forensic accounting guys to look at the books. Turns out that Treadwell is more than simply incompetent, he's shady as a counterfeit thousand dollar bill. Susan was so angry, she confronted him with the evidence. She didn't even wait until I got back. I'm a little disappointed. I would've liked to have seen the little piss-

217

ant squirm up-close."

"What happened?" I ask as I fasten his other cufflink.

"I think I may have mentioned Treadwell is not the brightest in the bunch. He tried to claim that Anita, one of the other associates, was sexually harassing him. He conveniently forgot Florida is a two-party state. He needed permission to tape any conversations with her. He even tried to manufacture several recordings against her."

"Seriously? What a dirt bag!" I exclaim.

"Well, the good news is he's as bad at being a criminal as he was being an attorney. He didn't bother to check Anita's docket at the time of the alleged incident. It turns out that when he made the so-called 'incriminating' tape, Anita was actually in an on-the-record-mediation with me, complete with a recorded video transcript and several witnesses, including the mediator — who acknowledged her exceptional performance as an associate."

"Is that unusual?" I ask, unfamiliar with the process.

"Mediation is a bit different from trial work and we usually try to disappear into the process a little more. So, yeah to be acknowledged in the process is pretty exceptional. In this case, if Treadwell decides to pursue anything, being on the record will help her, for sure."

"Do you think he would really do anything?"

Mark sighs heavily as he shrugs. "Who knows? Nothing that kid has done in his whole career has made any sense. He might try to take advantage of the notoriety Hunters Crossing is getting from the Florida Bar to press his case. I hope not. The award is long-overdue recognition for some really good attorneys who have their hearts in the right place."

I stand on my tiptoes and kiss Mark, taking care not to smudge my makeup. I guess if there is any advantage to having hair that's less than a half an inch long, it's that your eyes look huge and your earrings become the star attraction.

"Have I told you recently how proud I am of you? Having Hunters Crossing be named one of the Top Ten Places to Practice Law in Florida While Making a Difference is a huge deal. I'm proud of you for sticking to your guns. It's great that they're going to have an annual law school scholarship related to the honor."

"It was difficult to buck the trend and go into our quarterly meeting with only my suspicions and the data Isaac and his forensic team had uncovered. If I was wrong, I stood the chance of unjustly taking someone's career down along with my own."

"What happens to him now?" I rub a knot of tension out of Mark's shoulders.

He shrugs. "It's not up to me anymore. It's been turned over to the disciplinary branch of the bar association and I have no idea if any law enforcement officials are seriously looking at charges. I'm just relieved he's not dealing with clients anymore." Mark rubs his temples. "Unfortunately, this means we have to hire a new associate in a hurry, as soon as I get back into town."

"I'm sorry, personnel issues are always a pain," I commiserate.

"It seems as if everything has blown up because I decided to go on this trip. I got a text from Tristan marked urgent too. That's not usually his style."

I fish my cell phone out of my pocket and look at

the messages. "That's weird, I don't have any messages. I don't think we missed any rehearsals."

Mark makes a face at me. "Remind me again how I ended up officiating this wedding? Don't get me wrong, I like Mitch and Jessica, but don't you think it should have been someone else?"

"As nearly as I can tell, it happened sometime between Mitch's friend Stuart being kicked in the kidneys by a horse and you mentioning to Jessica's dad you are licensed to practice law here. By the way, who takes the California bar exam on a dare?"

Mark flushes a deep shade of red. "Okay, so I'll admit Susan and I might've been a little competitive in our younger days."

I raise an eyebrow. "You think? Anyway, Jessica's grandpa usually does these, but he can't walk her up the aisle and do the ceremony, so you got drafted."

"Shelby, does Jessica know I've never actually officiated a wedding before?" Mark frets.

"Yeah, they know." I respond with a hitch of my shoulder. "Jessica doesn't care. She thinks you sound regal. They just want their friends around and they aren't aiming for perfection."

"That's good, because they won't get perfection from me," Mark says with a gust of laughter. "This may be the strangest wedding in history."

Ketki is practically vibrating with excitement as we stand at the end of the makeshift aisle in the middle of the vineyard "When I told Jessica I didn't want to be a flower girl, she didn't tell me I'd be walking a dog up the aisle."

"I know, it's cool," I respond, as I reach down to give the German Shepherd, Hope, a quick scratch.

"I get to wear jeans," she adds, "*and* sparkly earrings. It's weird."

"Jessica said you were casually chic." I reply.

"Still weird," insists Ketki.

Jessica's grandfather, Walter, smiles down at Ketki and whispers, "It could've been a whole lot weirder. She could've done one of her belly dances up the aisle. She likes to pretend like I don't know — but, I've known for years."

Jessica laughs out loud as she kisses her grandfather on the cheek, "Why didn't you say something before? That would've been a totally epic idea."

Walter shakes his head in bemusement as he replies, "That's exactly why. We may not be in a formal house of the Lord, but it's still a wedding. Can you at least pretend it's not a variety show to make your grandma happy, please?"

Jessica hugs her grandpa. "I'll do my best."

Chapter Twenty-Four

Mark

To say this moment is surreal doesn't exactly do it justice. Ivy is playing the flute and Declan is covering the acoustic guitar as my daughter and girlfriend are waiting to walk two very well behaved German shepherds up a path through a vineyard with the pageantry afforded a Royal wedding. Most eyes are on the happy couple, and rightly so. Yet, I can't help but watch my unusual little family.

I don't know Jessica well enough to know why she has taken a personal interest in Tayanita, but much like Shelby, my ex-wife seems to have been scooped up by this gang and folded into the group. Shelby could've made this process very awkward, but she has chosen not to make an issue of the past. Instead, the women seem to be going out of their way to set aside their differences to make things work for Ketki's sake. Jessica is taking full advantage of Tayanita's eye for precise detail and computer skills by placing her in charge of the sound system. Tayanita smiles at Ketki as she gives her the cue to begin walking up the aisle with Shelby.

Although it's only been seven months since Shelby walked into my life, it seems like a lifetime ago.

Everything in my life has changed. Even though the cancer has been ugly, distressing and sometimes heart-stoppingly scary, Shelby has brought a spirit of wholeness and peace I've never had in my life.

As I watch Ketki confidently manage the big German Shepherd, I marvel in the changes in her as well. Although she'll likely never be fully comfortable connecting with other people, it seems to be easier for her to hold eye contact and engage in full conversation, instead of simply spouting a list of questions. Maybe it's wishful thinking, but it feels to me as if Ketki is becoming more confident in her ability to read the world around her. I think Shelby's faith in her has a lot to do with it.

Hope, the first German Shepherd, parks herself at Mitch's feet and doesn't move, despite valiant attempts at intervention from dog trainers from Mitch's facility, Devon and Riley. Finally, Ketki just gives up and sits on the ground next to Hope.

After the drama is resolved, Shelby begins walking up the aisle with her dog, Lexicon. She is so self-conscious about her short hair, but I don't think she understands how beautiful her smile is. Her eyes, bright with tears, are stunningly gorgeous. When she sees me tear up, she sighs and murmurs, "Oh my, this is better than a Hollywood movie."

Jessica is watching our interaction and comments dryly, "I think these two forgot whose wedding this is."

Shelby flushes with embarrassment. "I'm so sorry Jess, I didn't mean to take away from your day."

Standing beside me, Mitch smirks as he comments, "Shelby, don't worry about it, she's pulling your leg. Jessica would match up every last person in the whole state of California if she could. She is a certified, dyed-in-the-wool matchmaker."

This time, it's Jessica's turn to blush as she confirms, "It's totally true." She turns to the audience gathered at her wedding and teasingly asks, "Okay, so who's next?"

Ketki springs to her feet and raises her hand. "I know, I know!"

Mitch puts his hand on Ketki's shoulder. "I hesitate to ask this, but what do you know?"

Ketki gives Mitch a look which clearly indicates she believes he has asked the dumbest question ever invented. "I know who's getting married next."

Mitch gamely plays along. "Really? How do you know?"

Again, Ketki nails him with her famous look of total exasperation ring, "Shelby sleeps in my dad's bed."

The crowd erupts in awkward laughter. Ketki looks confused. "What's so funny? It's true, I swear," she insists stridently. "At first Shelby was really sick and my dad has the best bed in the house. He took really good care of her until she got better."

Ketki's impassioned, yet completely inappropriate defense of me makes me want to simultaneously laugh out loud and disappear into a deep hole in the ground.

I lean over to Mitch and whisper, "Sorry … not sure what to do here —"

Mitch shrugs as he replies with a bemused grin, "No problem here, it's riveting stuff."

Ketki glares at Mitch as she continues, "Anyways, like I was sayin', Shelby stayed with us for a long time because it's hard to make cancer go away. Pretty soon, Dad was doing things like telling Shelby stories about his job and singing to the radio. He would find silly reasons to buy her presents. You know, like it's Thursday. I'm telling you, I'd be trying to talk to my dad and he would have a goofy smile on his face and not be paying any attention to what I had to say. That's why I know that Shelby and my dad will be next."

Mitch seems to be stunned into speechlessness for a minute, so Walter comes to his rescue.

"I can see why you would think your dad might want to marry Shelby, but there are lots of grown-up decisions to be made," the pastor cautions, with a gentle smile.

"Oh, I know all about grown-up stuff, we had this conversation when it came to my *other* mom," Ketki huffs. "I know, being a grown up is hard. Still, I don't think anything is harder than dying of cancer and Shelby is all done with that, the doctor said. Okay, she still has to go to the doctor, but she's pretty safe now. I mean, she's not going to die tomorrow. Okay, technically, she may die tomorrow — did you know four people out of one hundred thousand people die for absolutely no reason at all every day? — but that's not the plan. Shelby needs to marry my dad just like in the movies."

Tayanita tries to intercede, "Ketki, I know you love Shelby, but I don't know if you can go around planning other people's lives —"

Ketki is laser focused on making her point now, "Dad — you love Shelby, right?"

I glance at Jessica and mouth the words, "I'm sorry."

"No, this is awesome!" Jessica asserts. "It's like dinner theater at my own wedding. I can't wait to see how it turns out."

The crowd titters again as I walk over to where Ketki is standing. I hitch her up on my hip. "Ki, I'm not sure this is the time and place for this. We are smack in the middle of someone else's wedding," I suggest.

Ketki glances over to Jessica in distress. "You asked us to tell you, right?"

Jessica nods in confirmation. "I totally did, although I wasn't expecting the answer to be quite this exciting." Jessica sinks down into a wrought-iron bench and pulls Walter down next to her.

I study Shelby's body language to see if I can glean any clues, but she looks a little befuddled by the whole conversation.

"Ketki, you might want to hang on tight. I've got to do a little maneuvering here. I wasn't exactly planning to do this right this second," I warn as I start to pat down my pockets.

"Dad, put me down. I'm not a baby. People will be taking pictures," Ketki pleads.

"You're right, I always forget how big you are. After all, you're ten now. You're practically a senior citizen —"

"I am not!" she exclaims with a horrified gasp. "Oh, you probably meant that as a joke, didn't you?"

"We should probably wrap this up so Jessica and Mitch can get married sometime before you go to college. Will you go get Shelby for me?"

"What do I do with Lexicon?" she asks with a puzzled look.

"You could hand him to Devon," I suggest.

"Okay," she responds as she runs down the aisle toward Shelby.

"Where's the popcorn when you need it?" Marcus quips.

"I don't know, but I do know this isn't the safe, standard ceremony Jessica promised me," Walter teases with an exaggerated wink.

He turns to his wife. "Are you doing all right, honey?"

"Why yes! Walt, this is more exciting than my favorite afternoon soaps. Now, please move out of the way so I can see." Walter promptly leans back on the bench to give his wife a better view.

Now that I've had a chance to get myself a little organized in all the chaos, I step forward and kneel down on one knee in front of Shelby as I ask, "Shelby Lynne Lyons, I love you, will you marry me?" I hold out a handcrafted engagement ring designed to resemble a dream catcher.

Shelby immediately puts her hand out for me to place the ring on as she whispers, "Yes, I love you too. I am ready to marry you and be your wife."

I make an exaggerated gesture of wiping sweat from my brow. Ketki hands me a crumpled up tissue.

"As you say, Mark, love is more than skin deep," she whispers tearfully.

Shelby pulls me up to a standing position and wraps her arms around my neck and kisses me deeply. This elicits a round of hoots and hollers from the crowd. Shelby breaks away and hides her face as she laughs.

Ketki pulls on Shelby's skirt as she asks, "Are you marrying me too? Are you going to be my mom?"

Shelby grins widely. "I sure am. I'm excited to call

you my daughter." She carefully draws Ketki into a tight hug and kisses the top of her head.

Ketki high-fives me as she exclaims, "Did you hear that, Dad? We're getting married. Can we have dogs at our wedding too?"

"I don't know, we'll have to work out the details later," I answer. "Why don't we let Jessica and Mitch get married now, since this is supposed to be their big day?"

"Okay, but it's not my fault. She asked the question," protests Ketki.

Jessica stands up and carefully rearranges her wedding dress. She motions for Ketki to approach. When Ketki does, she gives her a gentle hug. "I'm glad you shared your dad's love story with us. It felt so special to be part of this day."

She helps Walter stand up and instructs, "Grandpa, I think I'm going to need you to step in here. Mark looks a little preoccupied."

"Oh, you are a sneaky one … I should've known you never intended to have the fancy lawyer in charge of your ceremony. Why would you give an old man a heart attack like that? You guys were just mean!"

"Gramps, if I had told you that you were in charge of both jobs you would've worried yourself silly about how you would do both things. This way, you got both jobs done just fine."

"But I didn't plan for your ceremony —" Walter demurs.

"Balderdash! You've been planning for my ceremony since I was five," Jessica counters with a laugh. "Just give Mitch and me the abbreviated version. I didn't get a chance to eat breakfast this morning because I lost my contact lens and I'm starving."

Walter reaches into his jacket pocket and retrieves a lengthy list and unfurls it with a dramatic flourish. "I might have a few things to say —"

Wilma shakes her head at Walter as she comments, "You are so busted."

I can't recall a time I've ever been so happy to sit down. I was honored to be asked to officiate Jessica and Mitch's wedding, but I just don't think they understood what they could've been in for. Cherokee weddings are quite different from Christian weddings. I didn't want to say anything, but privately, I was a little worried that I might get blankets and vases mixed up with unity candles and rings. When you add that together with inclusion of dogs, kids and the unexpected absence of Mitch's best man, Stuart, it was probably better to have an experienced pastor at the helm.

Shelby nudges me in the ribs as she quietly whispers, "Did you know any of this was going to happen?"

I shake my head. "No, I didn't. I think our daughter played us like an eighteen-piece orchestra."

Shelby admires her shiny new ring as she declares, "I can't find it in my heart to be upset about that, can you?"

I chuckle softly. "No not really."

Walter pointedly clears his throat as he chastises, "I thought that you lovebirds were done hogging the spotlight. Are we ready to start my granddaughter's wedding?"

"Yes, sir," I respond sitting straighter in my chair.

"Very well. Ladies and gentlemen there was a time when I thought we would never be here on a day like today. In fact, there was a time I thought I'd never see my dear Jessica again. We had been estranged for years. By some miracle, Mitch managed to bring my beautiful, headstrong granddaughter home in one piece. Not only that, Mitch and his heroic dogs saved my Wilma from certain death."

Mitch swallows hard as he acknowledges the compliment, "Honored to do it."

Walter winks at the audience. "Of course there was that time you almost broke her heart and I was tempted to shoot you in the buttocks with a .22 just to show you what real pain feels like."

"Grandpa, short and sweet — remember short and sweet," reminds Jessica with an exasperated sigh.

"Oh, all right, Buttercup. I suppose that means you don't want me to tell them that your love story with Mitch reminds me so much of my own with Wilma?"

Tayanita hands Jessica a Kleenex just as her tears start to overflow, "Oh Gramps, I didn't want you to get started on all that because once you start, where do you stop?"

"You start with the fact that you love that man with your whole heart, that's where you start. Hopefully, by the grace of God, that's where you finish too."

Jessica turns to Mitch and grabs both of his hands. "I never knew that day when I took a very sick, skinny, hopeless German Shepherd in to see you that it would not only be Hope you would save that day, it would be me. You saved all of my hopes, dreams and aspirations. You helped me discover who I was, who was important and what I was passionate about. You reminded me about what was important in my life. You brought my family back together and helped me create a new one. You helped me believe in myself again — something I hadn't been able to do in a long time. I'm so happy that I'll finally be your wife."

Mitch smiles down at Jessica. "Jess, you weren't the only one who was hopeless when we met. I had given up the idea I would ever find love after losing Nora."

A startled gasp goes through the crowd at the mention of Mitch's former girlfriend.

Jessica hears the commotion and looks up and smiles at everyone as she insists, "No, I'm good with the fact that he loved Nora. If he hadn't, he wouldn't have learned search and rescue and he wouldn't have been able to save my grandma and countless other people. Hope, Lexicon, Yuki and all the rest of the animals wouldn't have jobs and a purpose. Hope's Haven wouldn't exist. I think all of this happens for a reason and I'm grateful for the fact that he loved her first."

"Wow," Shelby mouths wordlessly beside me.

"Did I mention that my bride-to-be is pretty much perfect?" Mitch quips to the crowd.

"Jess, you have made it possible for me to rebuild my life and my dreams, and I can't imagine doing it all without you beside me I love you," Mitch declares as he holds tightly to her hands.

"Well then, Mitch and Jessica shall we get on with the official part of the ceremony?" Walter asks as he pulls out notes and his reading glasses.

"Grandpa, is all this necessary?" Jessica asks. "I thought that you were just planning to say a few sentimental words to make it all legal for us."

"I want to make sure I had all the highlights," Walter explains. "I don't want you guys complaining that I missed something crucial."

"Gramps, don't be silly. I love Mitch, and he loves me and we're here to tell the world about it. We're going to exchange rings, kiss awkwardly as we try not to embarrass ourselves and then we'll eat some cake. Does it really have to get any more complicated than that?"

Walter's heavy eyebrows draw together as he thinks for a moment. Finally, he says, "No, I suppose not. Any objections to that plan?"

Everyone in the audience looks at each other and shrugs.

Walter smiles at his granddaughter as he says, "Buttercup, it looks like you're in the clear. Congratulations, Mitch is a fine young man. As a minister in the state of Kansas and through several online ministries throughout the United States, I pronounce you man and wife, you may kiss your groom, Mrs. Mitch Campbell."

"Grandpa, what about our rings?" Jessica asks with a confused expression on her face.

Walter winks her as he says, "You said you wanted the ceremony short and sweet. I figured you guys could exchange rings after you're done eating cake."

Jessica sighs as she concludes, "Oh … Gramps, you forgot the wedding rings in the hotel room, didn't you?"

"I'm old. I can't be expected to remember everything — my cell phone died," Walter explains. "Now are you going to kiss your husband or what?"

As the whole audience breaks out into enthusiastic applause, Shelby whispers in my ear, "I don't know if this means we should automatically book this guy as our minister or make sure we never call him?"

I shrug. "I don't know, I can't decide either. One thing is for certain, if we put Walter in charge of our wedding, it won't be boring."

Epilogue

Shelby

"How in the world did you talk Dad into letting me do this?" Ketki asks me. "He's usually pretty adamant about extra holes in my body."

"Does the word surprise ring any bells?" I answer vaguely.

"Oh, so you're just not telling him — otherwise known as lying." Ketki confronts me in her usual blunt way.

"Well, you're technically right. It's partially a surprise and a little bit of not telling him. I'm two years cancer free and the PET scan looks great. He is out of town doing those trainings for the new branches of Hunters Crossing. So, instead of getting my dream catcher tattoo on my back like I originally planned, Rogue is going to put it on the outside of my thigh. My skin is less irritated there and the dermatologist said it would be okay."

"Really? I thought the doctors were totally against tattoos," Ketki replies.

"No, from what I understand it has a lot to do with the quality of ink. Ink'd Deep uses the highest quality medical grade tattoo ink, so the risk of allergic reaction or infection is a lot less," I explain

"You should see some of the videos out there on YouTube; it's a scary thing," Ketki remarks.

"That's why your mom is taking you to Ink'd Deep. You won't end up with some weird disease from mall-funk," Tayanita, declares with a shudder. "I know they don't use an autoclave to clean their equipment at the mall."

"Geez guys, I'm just getting my ears pierced it's not like I'm getting something major done." Ketki complains. "Sometimes, having two moms is a drag."

"Yeah, like when we take you out for your birthday and buy you twice as many video games?" I suggest.

"Or, when Shelby and I pool our resources to get you more expensive kicks or other cool stuff, I bet that's a real drag then too," Tayanita teases.

"Having two of us to help with boy problems — I bet that sucks too," I add facetiously.

Ketki turns red like every other twelve-year-old when you talk about boys. "It does suck!" she exclaims. "It's like you guys coordinate your advice or something. Most of the time it's almost exactly the same. What do you guys do, think with one brain?"

I laugh as I respond, "I wish I shared her brain. I've got a student in AP Biology and he's stretching my area of expertise. I could use Tayanita's smarts about now."

"How is that teaching position working out for you? I'd think it would be hard for you to work with kids with cancer after having fought it yourself," Tayanita asks with the insight of someone who works in healthcare. "Aren't you afraid fear will overtake you if you see people sick all the time?"

"Teaching in virtual classrooms has been great for me and the kids. However, I can't deny that there is some of that, especially when I see the kiddos get super sick from chemo. My stomach instinctively lurches out of sympathy. Yet, I think there's a lot to be said for being able to show them what it's like to be on the other side of it. I know as a skin cancer survivor, I won't ever be cured, only managed. Fortunately, the worst is behind me."

"I'm just sad that you and Dad won't have any babies. I always wanted to have a little sister," Ketki remarks.

I glance at her with surprise as I comment, "Really? This is the first time you've said anything. I didn't know you felt that way. I barely knew your dad at the time, so it was weird — but he made sure I sought the advice of an infertility specialist and harvested eggs before I started chemotherapy. There is still a chance of a baby for us although the doctor said it would be harder after chemotherapy."

Ketki rolls her eyes. "My dad is so strange. Only *he* would plan so far in advance. Still, I'm kinda glad he did."

I put my arm around Ketki. "You know your dad. He likes to say things are left up to fate and then he likes to push fate around."

Rogue comes back to her station with my dream catcher design all scaled down to fit my thigh. Before she places the stencil, I smile at her and announce, "I've got good news."

Rogue raises an eyebrow and asks, "Does this mean

you and Mister-Tall-Dark-and-Handsome have set a date to get married?"

I laugh out loud because Rogue asks me this every time I see her. It's been a huge bone of contention between Mark and me. I have a few outstanding bills from when I wasn't working I want to pay off before I get married. I'm almost done now that I have a job. It won't be too long before we can get married. Mark thinks I'm being ludicrous because he has the money several times over. That's not the point — it's about dignity. I spent too many years as a child begging for my existence to feel comfortable doing it now even though I know Mark doesn't see it that way.

"No, this is better — okay, maybe not better, but different," I acquiesce. "My latest cancer scan is completely clear."

Rogue lets out a huge victory cheer as she pulls Ketki up next to her. They stand on the back of the couch. Ketki manages to look both slightly terrified and majorly impressed. Rogue shouts across the showroom floor to Marcus. "Marcus! I have phenomenally great news breaking from Station Four."

Marcus answers, "Really? What kind of news is that, Ro?"

This time I'm prepared for the stomping and clapping which starts as a dull roar, but it takes Tayanita by surprise. Rogue laughs as she promises, "The best possible kind!"

The cheers grow louder.

Marcus eggs the customers on by challenging, "What do we do at Ink'd Deep if someone has good news?"

Rising to the challenge seemingly in unison, they all answer, "We celebrate!"

Ketki is watching the display with wide-eyed amazement. I've told her the story of how her dad and I met many times before, yet to see it unfold was a whole other thing. As if he can tell I'm thinking about him, my phone rings.

"Hello?" I yell over the din of noise.

"What are you doing?" Mark asks when he hears the commotion.

"Oh, just sharing a little good news," I admit. "Listen," I instruct as I place my phone on speaker phone.

"Stones, why don't you spill the good news —" Marcus tells Ketki.

"My mom had a special cancer scan and it didn't show any cancer. She doesn't have to have another test for a whole six months … and I'm twelve — that's almost like being a teenager!"

The whole shop is cheering and applauding. It's amazing how much my life has changed since the first time Marcus rang the bell for me.

I take the phone off of speakerphone as I gush to Mark, "Did you hear our daughter? She did so great!"

"I thought you and Tayanita were planning to take Ketki out for her birthday."

"We are," I confirm. "We have celebrations planned all around."

"Well, don't overdo it," Mark cautions. "I love you, Shelby. Tell Marcus to ring the bell extra loud. It seemed to work well last time."

My heart turns to mush over my fairy-tale life. I glance over at the girl who has stolen my heart. The fact that she is growing up at the speed of light is hard on all of us. Ketki holds up a pair of skull earrings with flashing eye sockets and shows them to me with an excited grin. I shake my head in disbelief as I sigh. I figure what Mark doesn't know won't hurt him. He *is* a sucker for presents after all…

THE END

Savannah's story continues in *Tough*..

Note from the Author

Dear Reader:

Thank you so much for reading *Love is More Than Skin Deep*. Preventing skin cancer is such an important message.

Mark and Shelby's story is just beginning. Savannah's emotional journey is next in *Tough*.

Savannah uprooted her entire life to be near her sister who has cancer.

Although, Savanna is thrilled to be reunited with Shelby, there are things about Savannah's past she isn't proud of.

Savannah is all about privacy and keeping to herself.

Unfortunately, the pushy coffee shop owner next door seems to have no boundaries.

Can Casey and Shelby survive the tough breaks to find tender love?

This deeply emotional contemporary romance will touch your heart.

Get *Tough* now in paperback, e-book version or read for free on Kindle Unlimited.

(*Tough* contains descriptive memories of sexual abuse. It may be disturbing to some.)

Thank you,

~ Mary

Because love matters, differences don't.

ACKNOWLEDGEMENTS

I WOULD LIKE TO acknowledge the author of the forward to this book, Judy Noble Cloud. In the current social media climate, it is extremely difficult to put yourself out there in anything except the most positive light. Hence the reason for dozens and dozens of programs for your phone to pre-filter your photographs before they ever hit the Internet. I cannot imagine the amount of bravery that it took her to post those raw, unfiltered photographs of her healing process. Yet, I cannot tell you how glad I am that she did. The raw honesty in those pictures are the basis for this story. After reading Judy's story on Facebook, I knew that I had to do my part to increase awareness. She has been so gracious in answering all of my questions, no matter how undignified and intrusive. Judy, I hope I did your story justice.

A huge thank you to Kathern Watts — who spent a great deal of time during the creation of this book underwater — both literally and figuratively. She has been elevated from a beta reader to a full-fledged research assistant and she does a phenomenal job for me. I cannot thank her enough.

As an author, your words are just your words until they are edited. I was honored to work with Lacie Redding and Jim Dodds on this project. Thank you very much for your contributions toward making me a stronger writer.

Kudos to Theodore Ashford who has been helping me create gorgeous marketing materials. Thank you for your time and artistry.

Thank you to all of my beta readers and my friends on the NaNoWriMo board. You all kept me going through some very difficult health challenges. Without you, I don't believe this book would've been possible. Write on. See you in November.

Rosemary McKenna, your last minute save was epic beyond belief. Thank you.

Antonia Trujillo — Thank you for trying so hard to keep me in one piece and breathing throughout this whole process. It is not an easy job.

Brandon, Justin and Leonard — as usual, you rock. Without you, I would be nothing.

ABOUT THE AUTHOR

I have been lucky enough to live my own version of a romance novel. I married the guy who kissed me at summer camp. He told me on the night we met that he was going to marry me and be the father of my children.

Eventually, I stopped giggling when he said it, and we've been married for more than thirty years. We have two children. The oldest is a Doctor of Osteopathy. He is across the United States completing his residency, but when he's done, he is going to come back to Oregon and practice Family Medicine. Our youngest son is now tackling high school and where he is an honor student. He is interested in becoming an EMT.

I write full time now. I have published more than thirty books and have several more underway. I volunteer my time to a variety of causes. I have worked as a Civil Rights Attorney and diversity advocate. I spent several years working for various social service agencies before becoming an attorney.

In my spare time, I love to cook, decorate cakes and of course, I obsessively, compulsively read.

I would be honored if you would take a few moments out of your busy day to check out my website,

MaryCrawfordAuthor.com. While you're there, you can sign up for my newsletter and get a free book. I will be announcing my upcoming books and giving sneak peeks as well as sponsoring giveaways and giving you information about other interesting events.

If you have questions or comments, please E-mail me at Mary@MaryCrawfordAuthor.com or find me on the following social networks:

Facebook: www.facebook.com/authormarycrawford

Website: MaryCrawfordAuthor.com

Twitter: www.twitter.com/MaryCrawfordAut

www.ingramcontent.com/pod-product-compliance
Lightning Source LLC
Chambersburg PA
CBHW032128180726

48284CB00002B/701